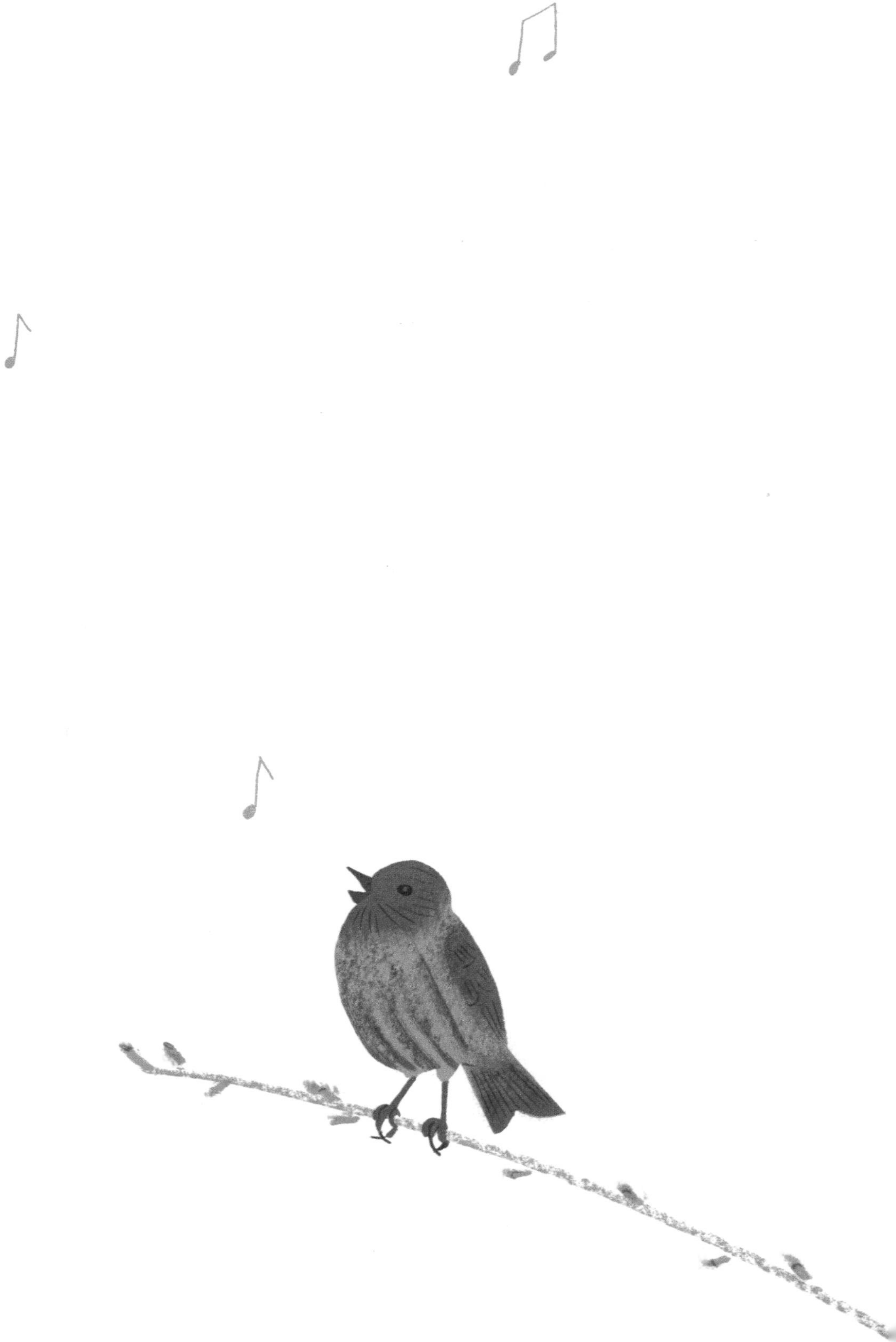

For Evan and Eli. — Sara

To my inspiring sons, H and M; my wonderful goddaughter, C;
and my three thrilling nephews, J, S and L. — Sophie

Published in Canada and the USA in 2019 by Groundwood Books

Groundwood Books / House of Anansi Press
groundwoodbooks.com

We gratefully acknowledge for their financial support of our publishing program the Canada Council for the Arts, the Ontario Arts Council and the Government of Canada.

Sophie Casson thanks the Conseil des arts et des lettres du Québec for its financial support.

Library and Archives Canada Cataloguing in Publication
Title: Helen's birds / Sara Cassidy ; drawn by Sophie Casson.
Names: Cassidy, Sara, author. | Casson, Sophie, illustrator.
Identifiers: Canadiana (print) 20189066873 | Canadiana (ebook) 20189066881 | ISBN 9781773060385 (hardcover) | ISBN 9781773060392 (EPUB) | ISBN 9781773060408 (Kindle)
Subjects: LCSH: Stories without words. | LCGFT: Graphic novels.
Classification: LCC PN6733 C37 H45 2019 | DDC j741.5/971–dc23

The illustrations were created in color pencil, Photoshop and pastel.
Design by Michael Solomon
Printed and bound in Malaysia

Canada Council for the Arts | Conseil des Arts du Canada
ONTARIO ARTS COUNCIL
CONSEIL DES ARTS DE L'ONTARIO
an Ontario government agency
un organisme du gouvernement de l'Ontario
With the participation of the Government of Canada
Avec la participation du gouvernement du Canada | Canada
MIX
Paper from responsible sources
FSC® C012700
www.fsc.org

HELEN'S BIRDS

SARA CASSIDY
DRAWN BY
SOPHIE CASSON

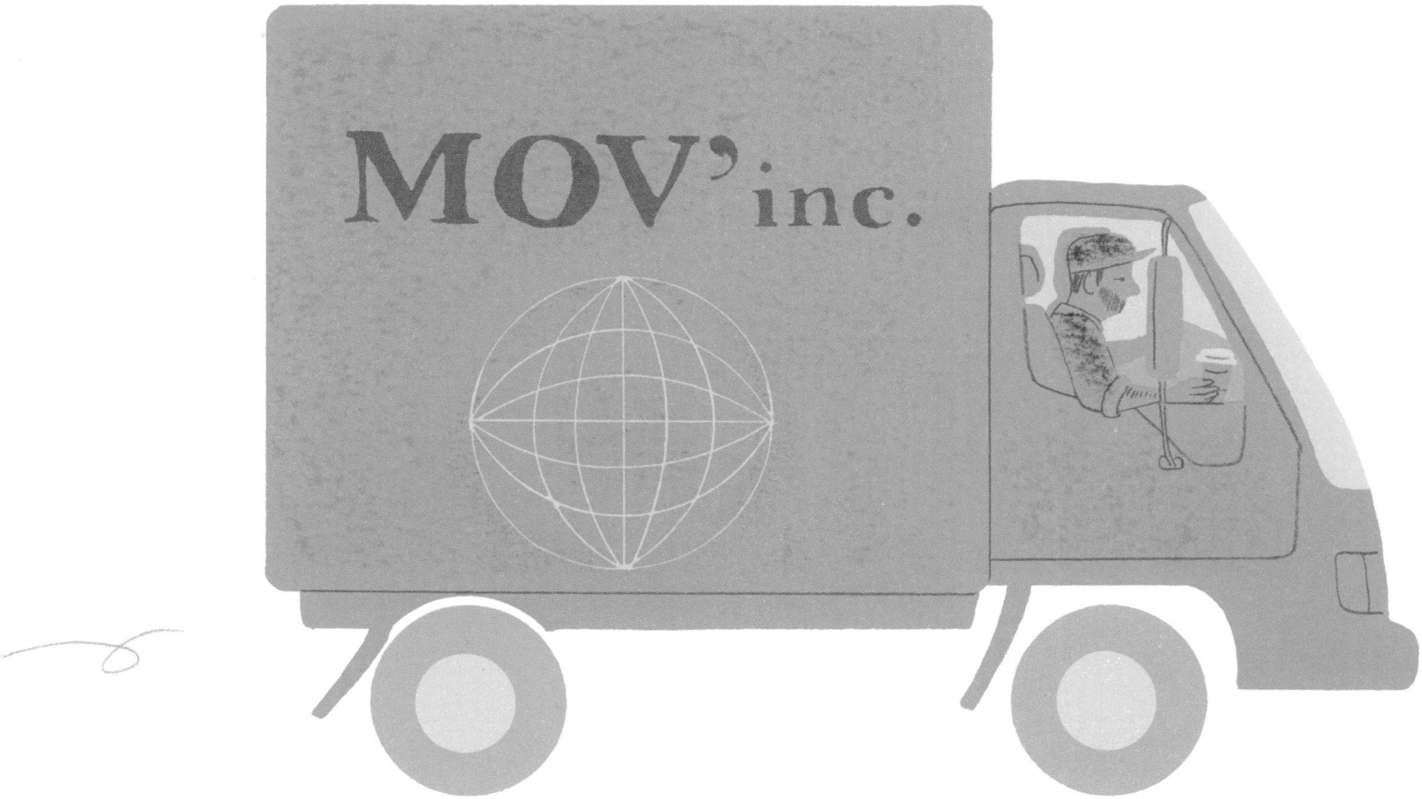
MOV' inc.

GROUNDWOOD BOOKS
HOUSE OF ANANSI PRESS
TORONTO BERKELEY

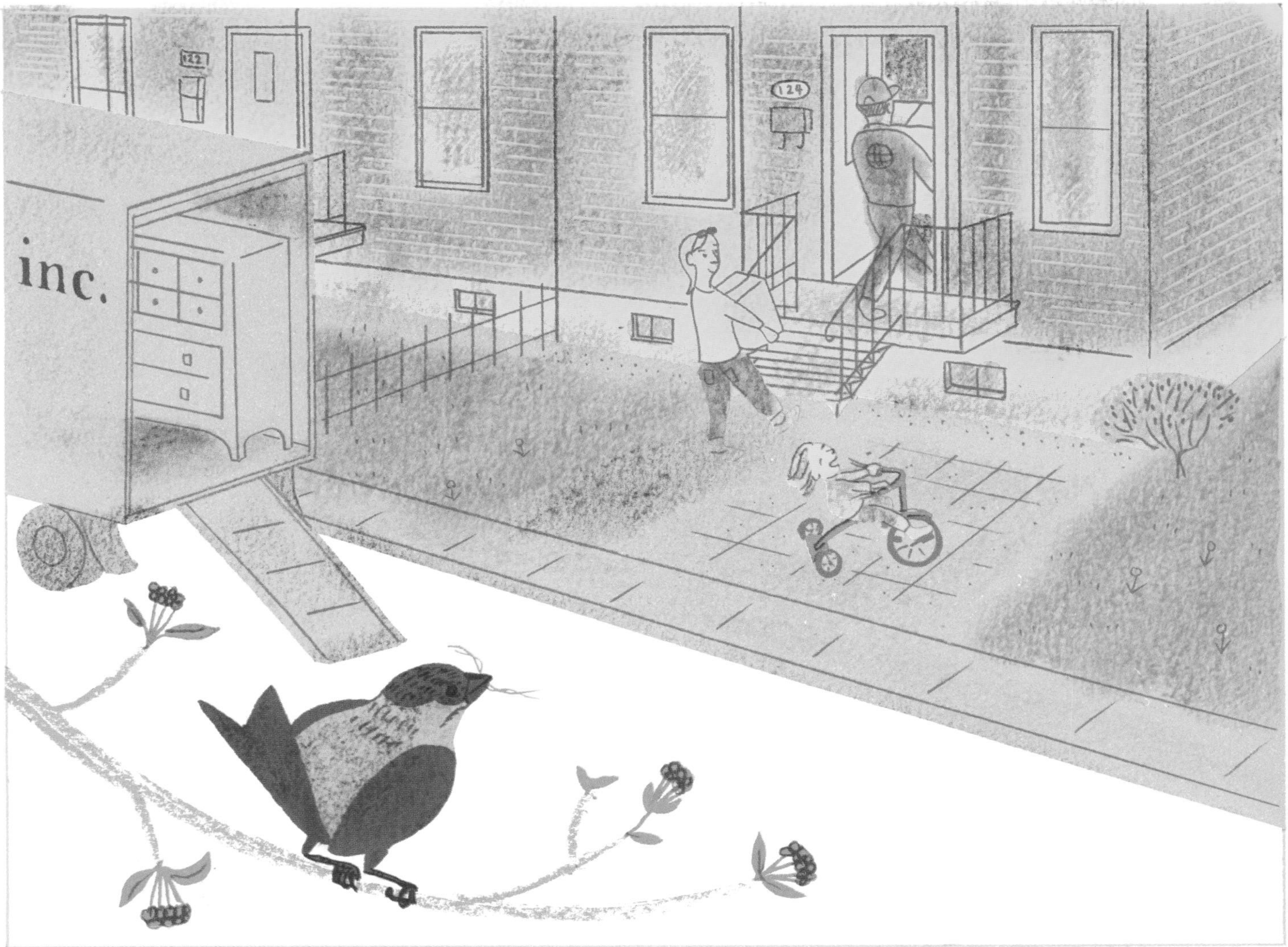
inc.
122
124

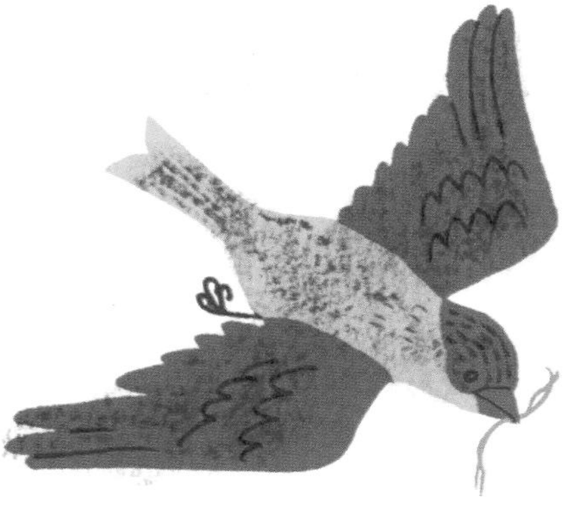

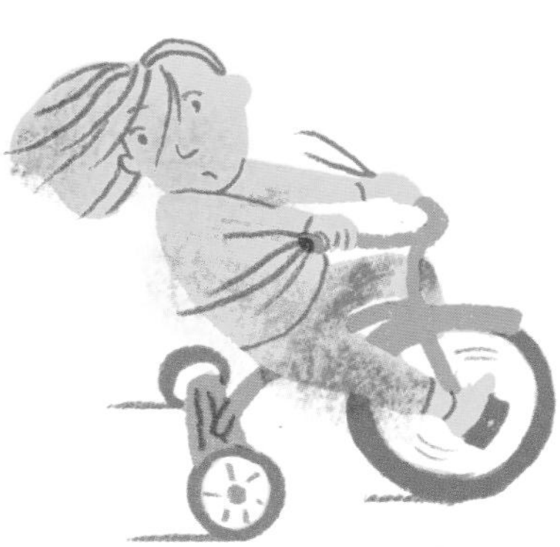

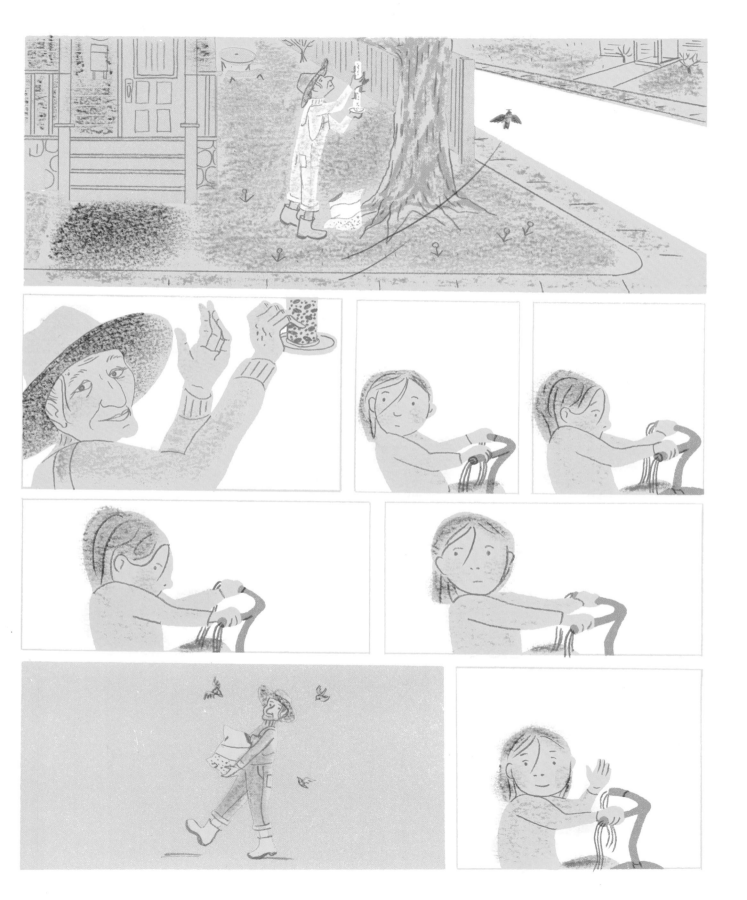

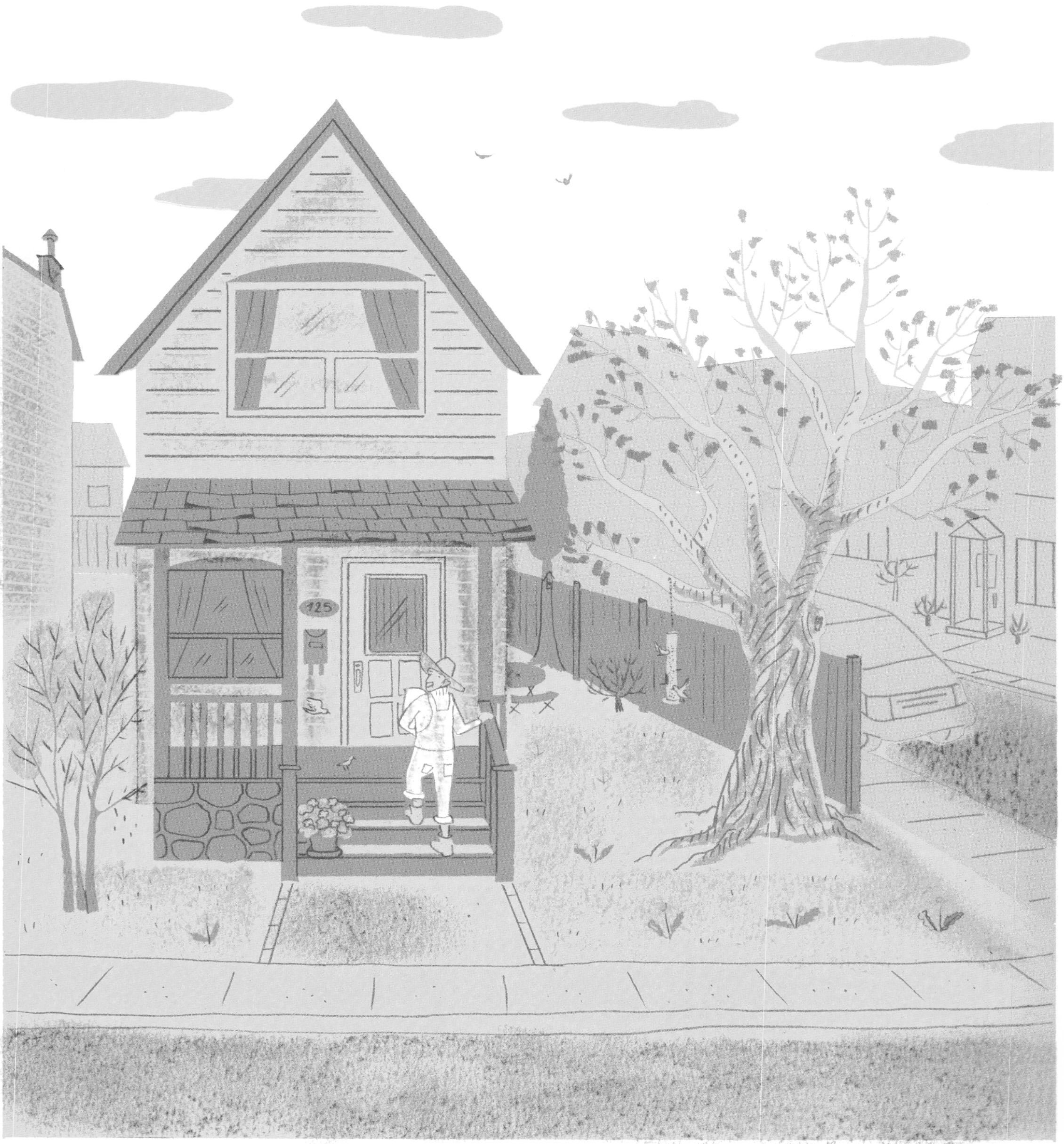
125

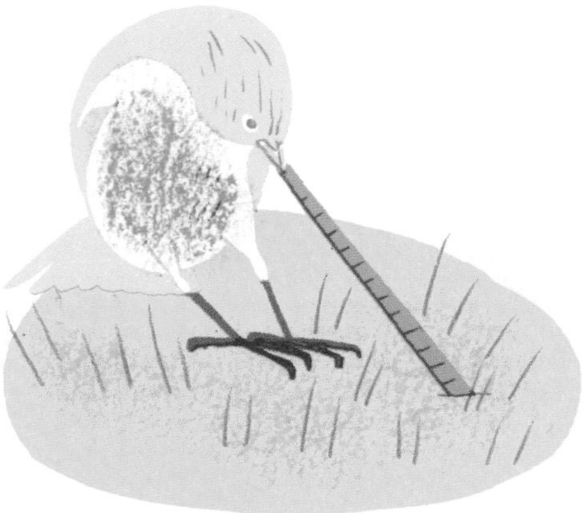

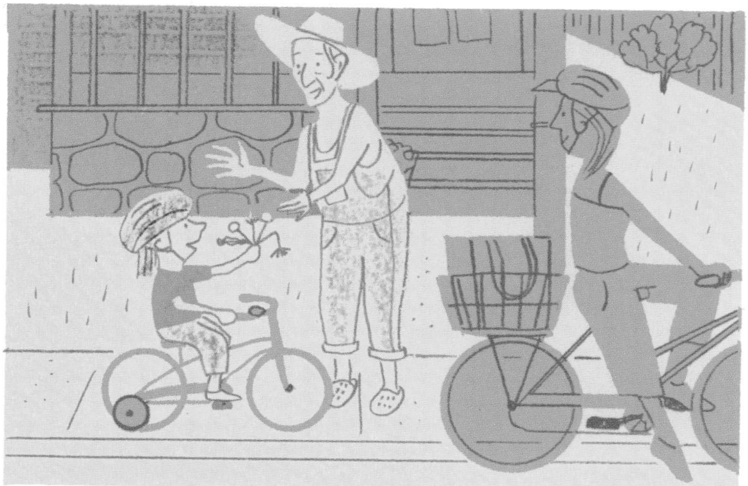

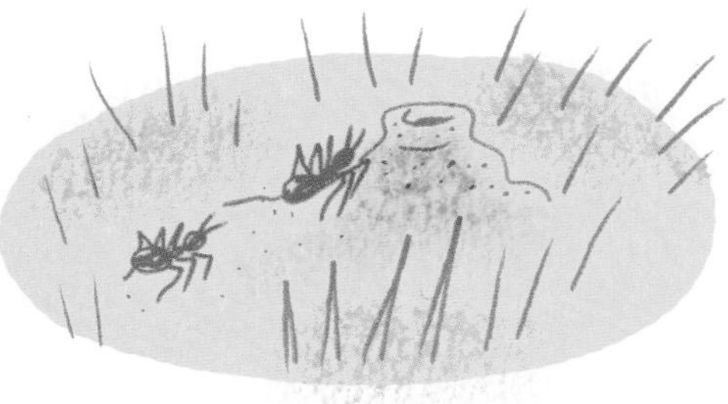

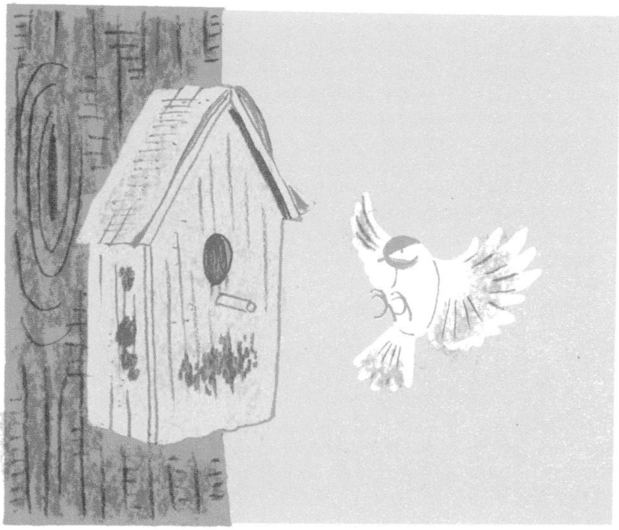

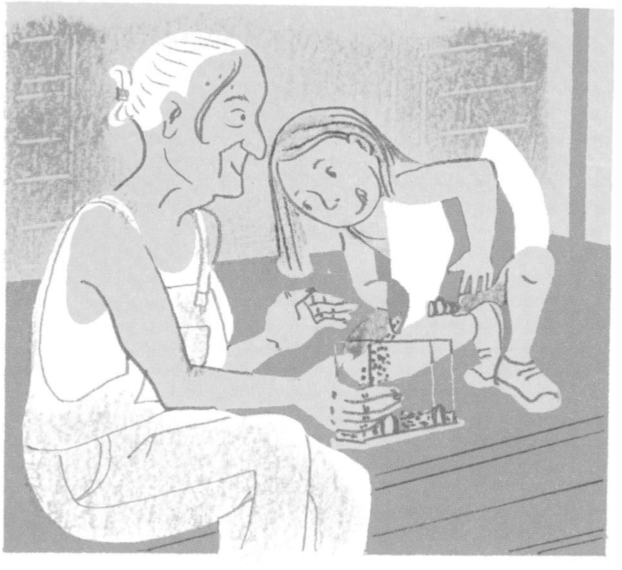

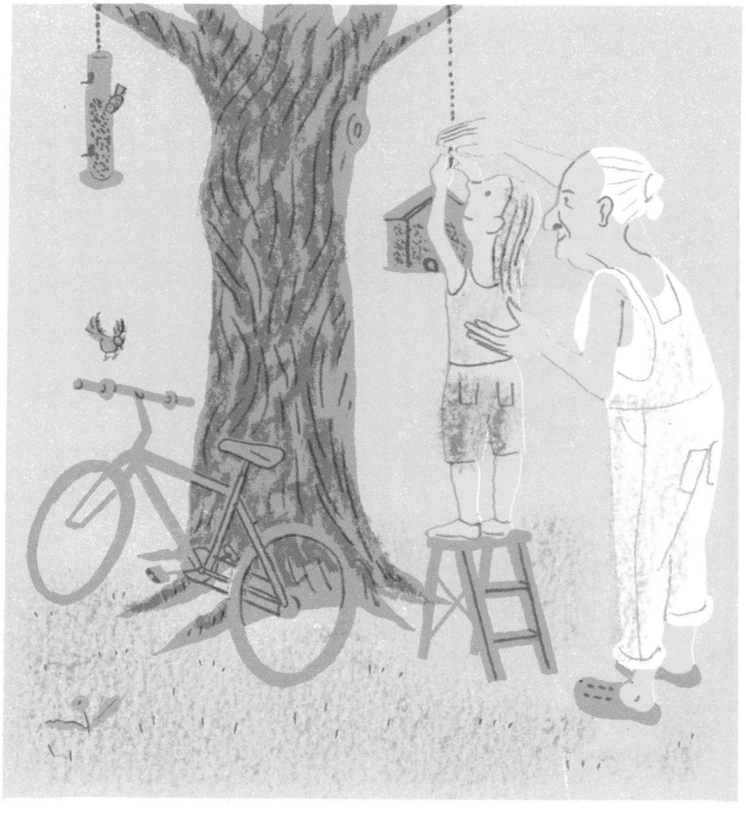

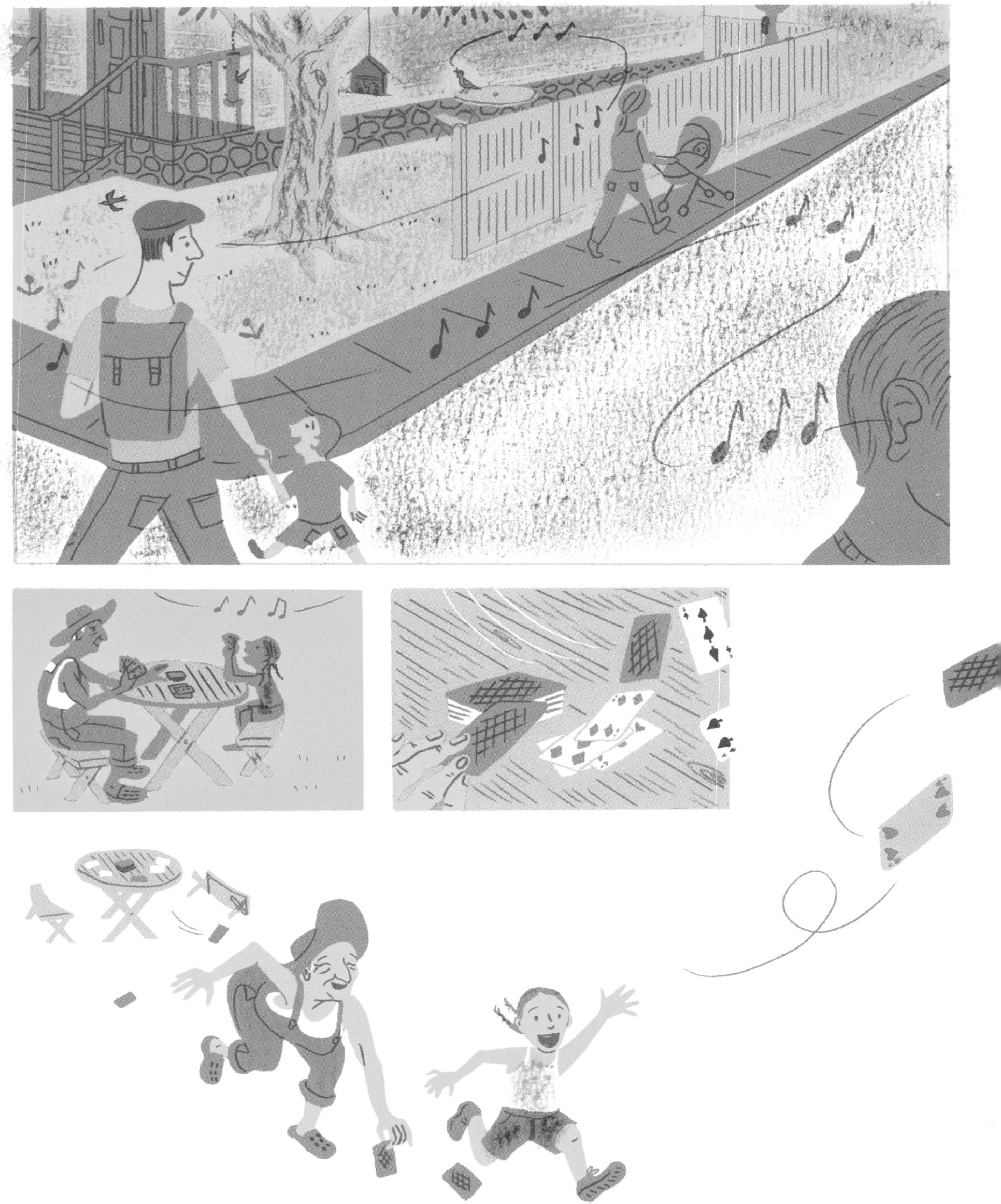

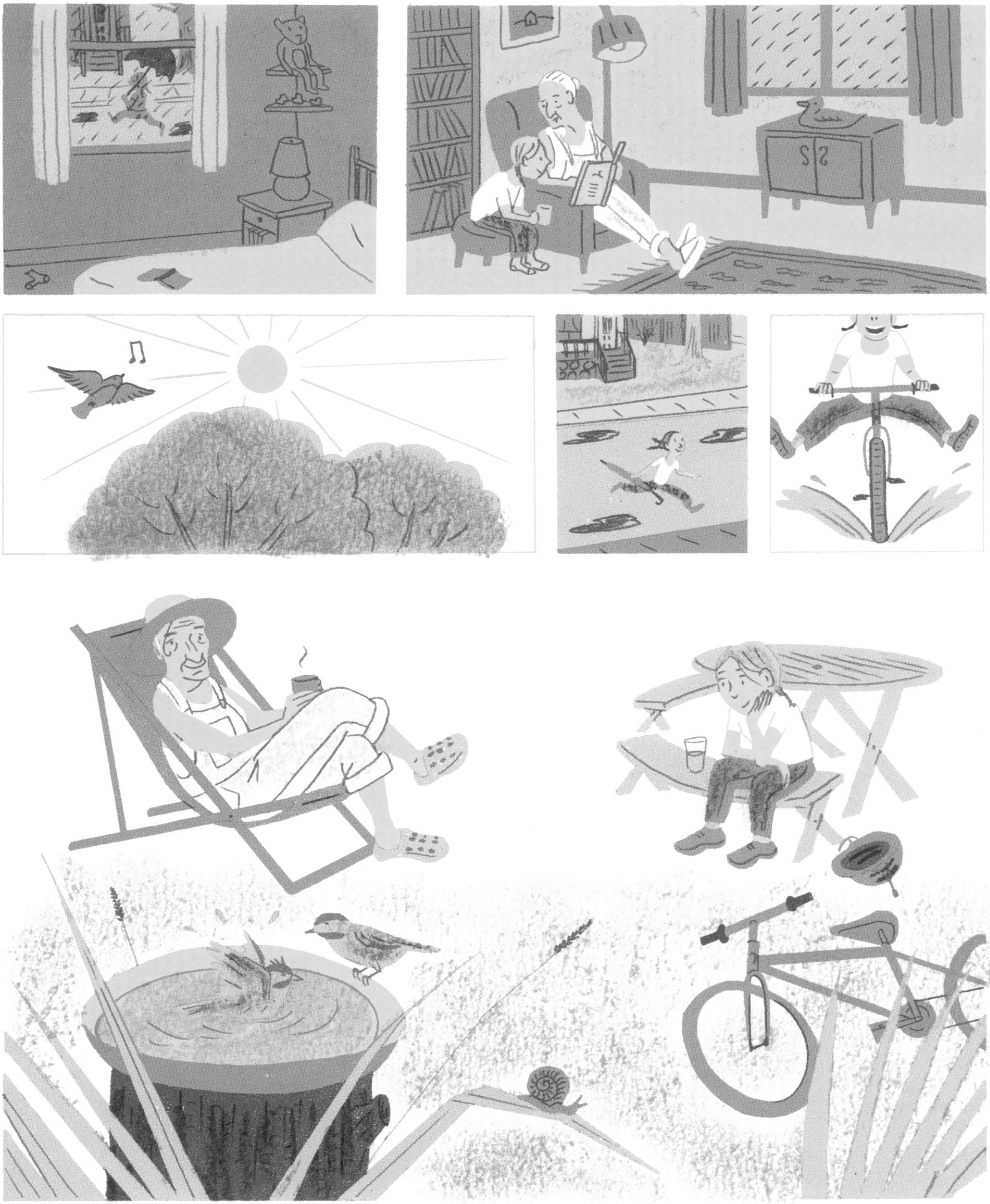

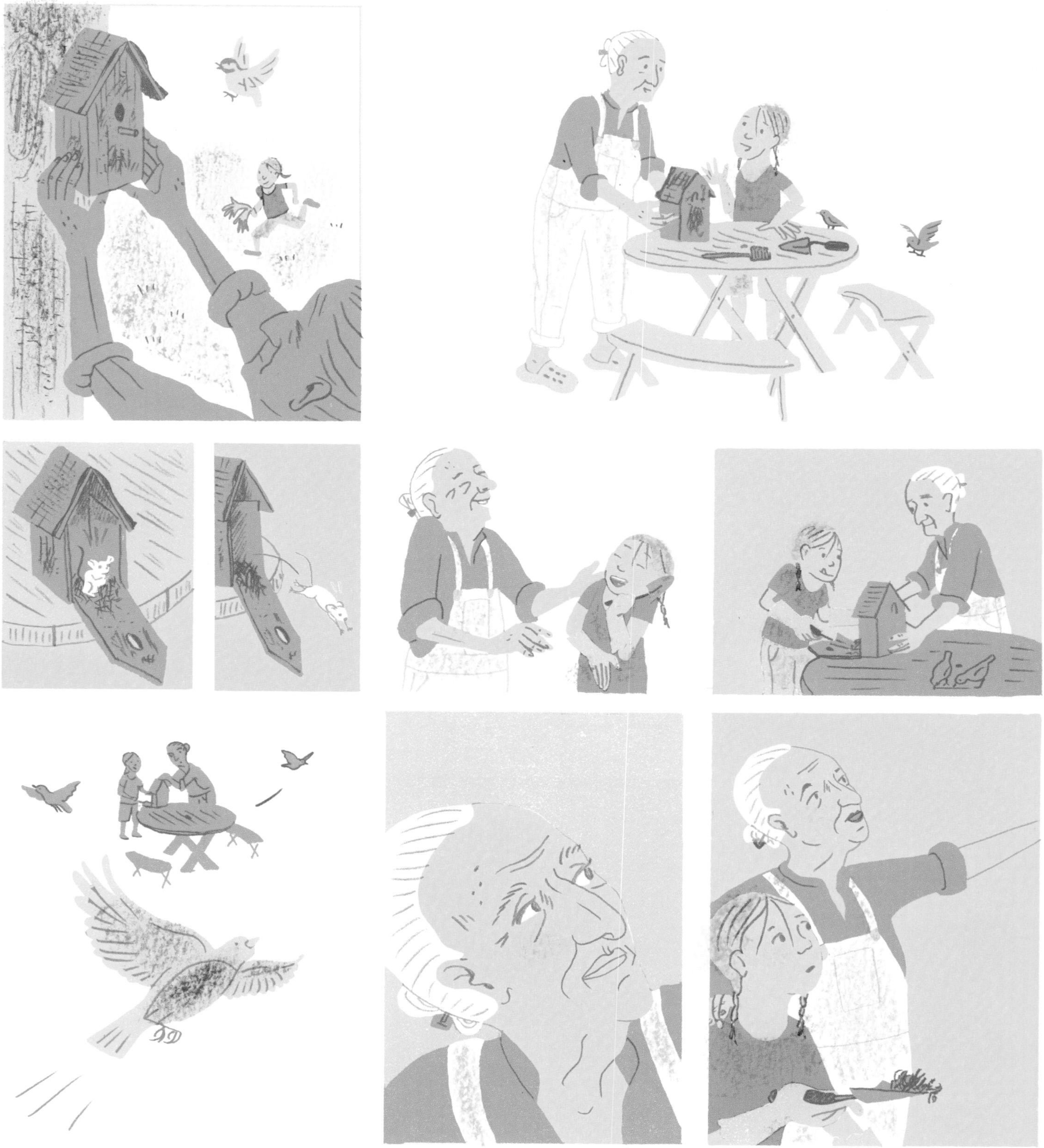

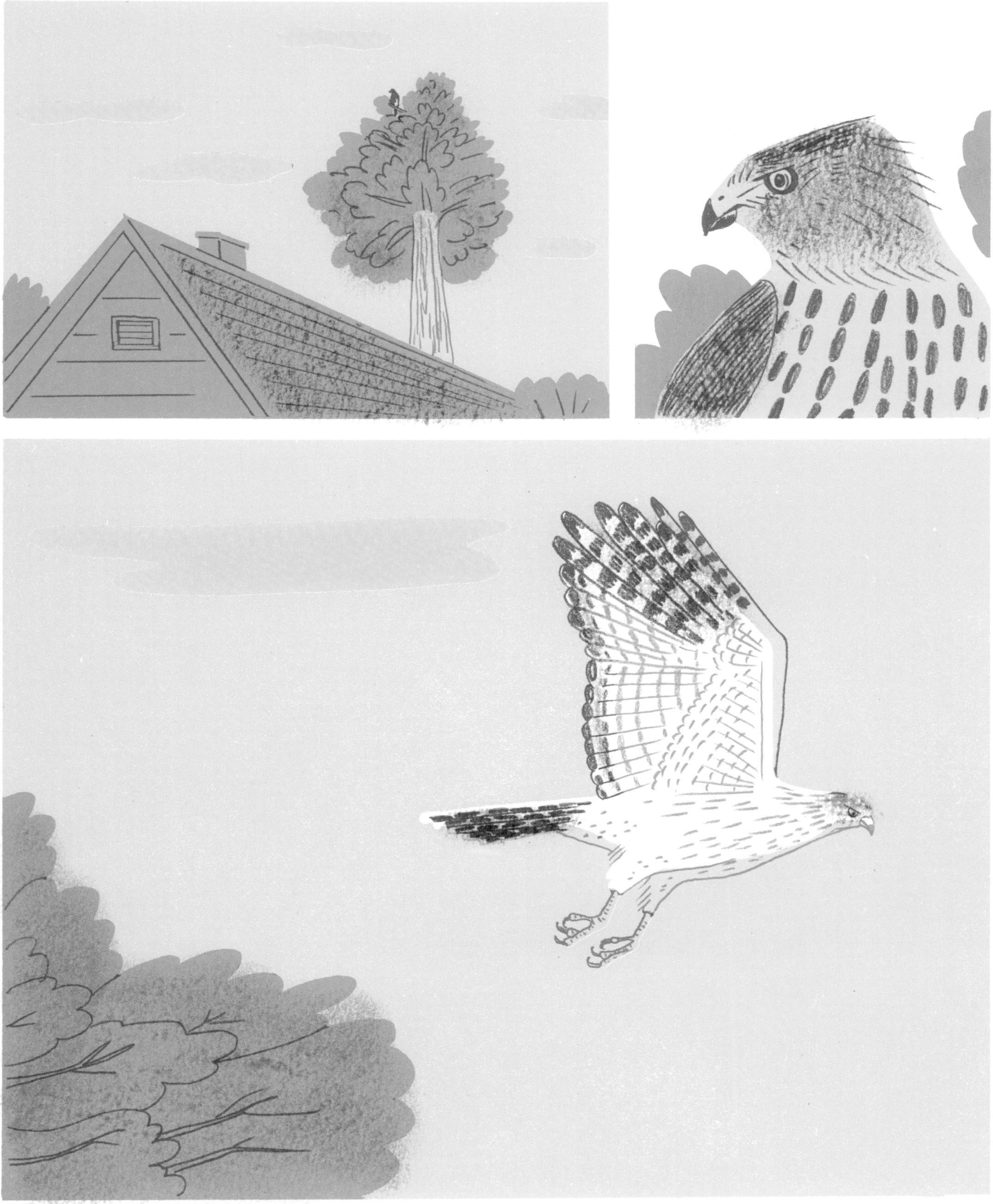

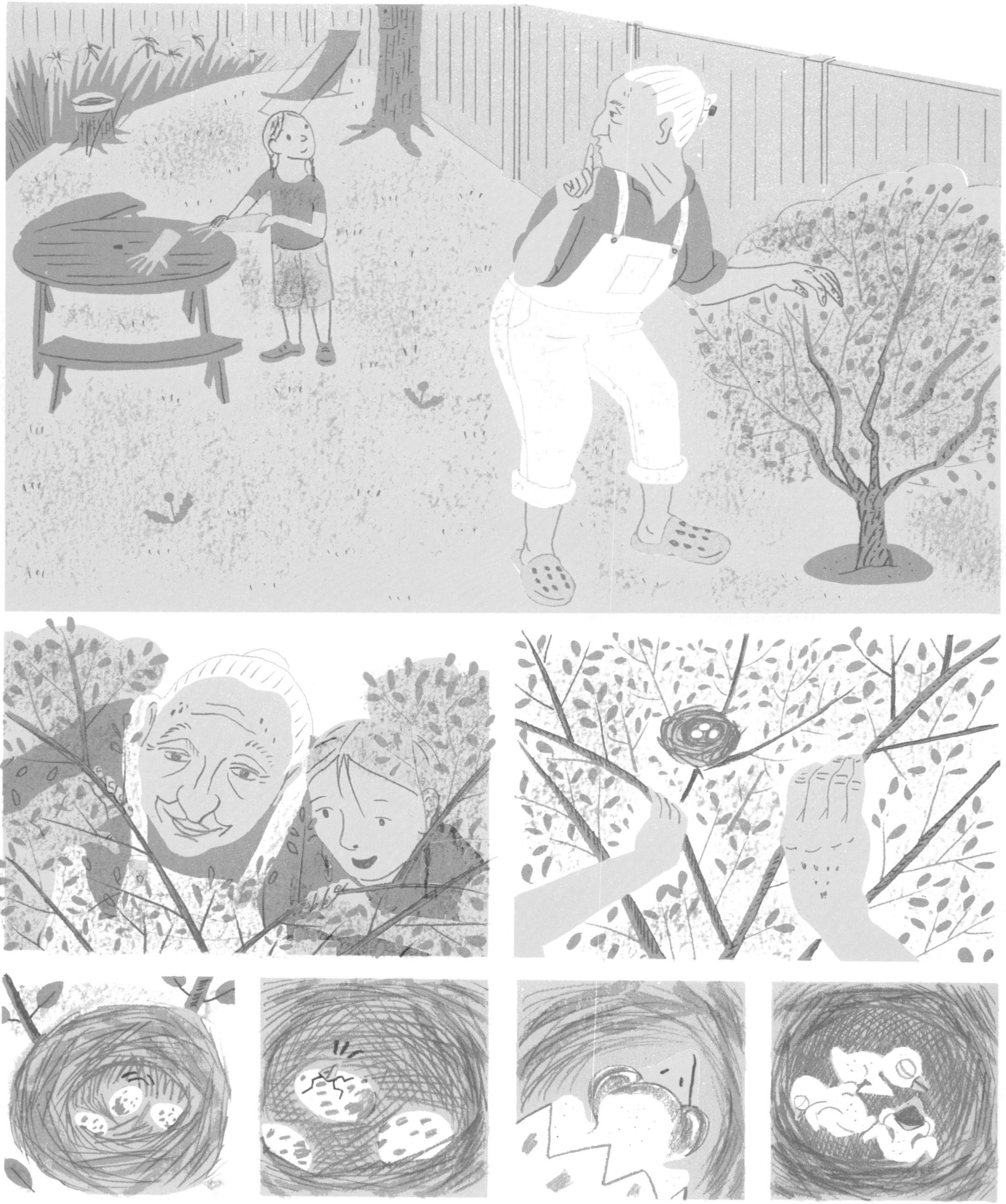

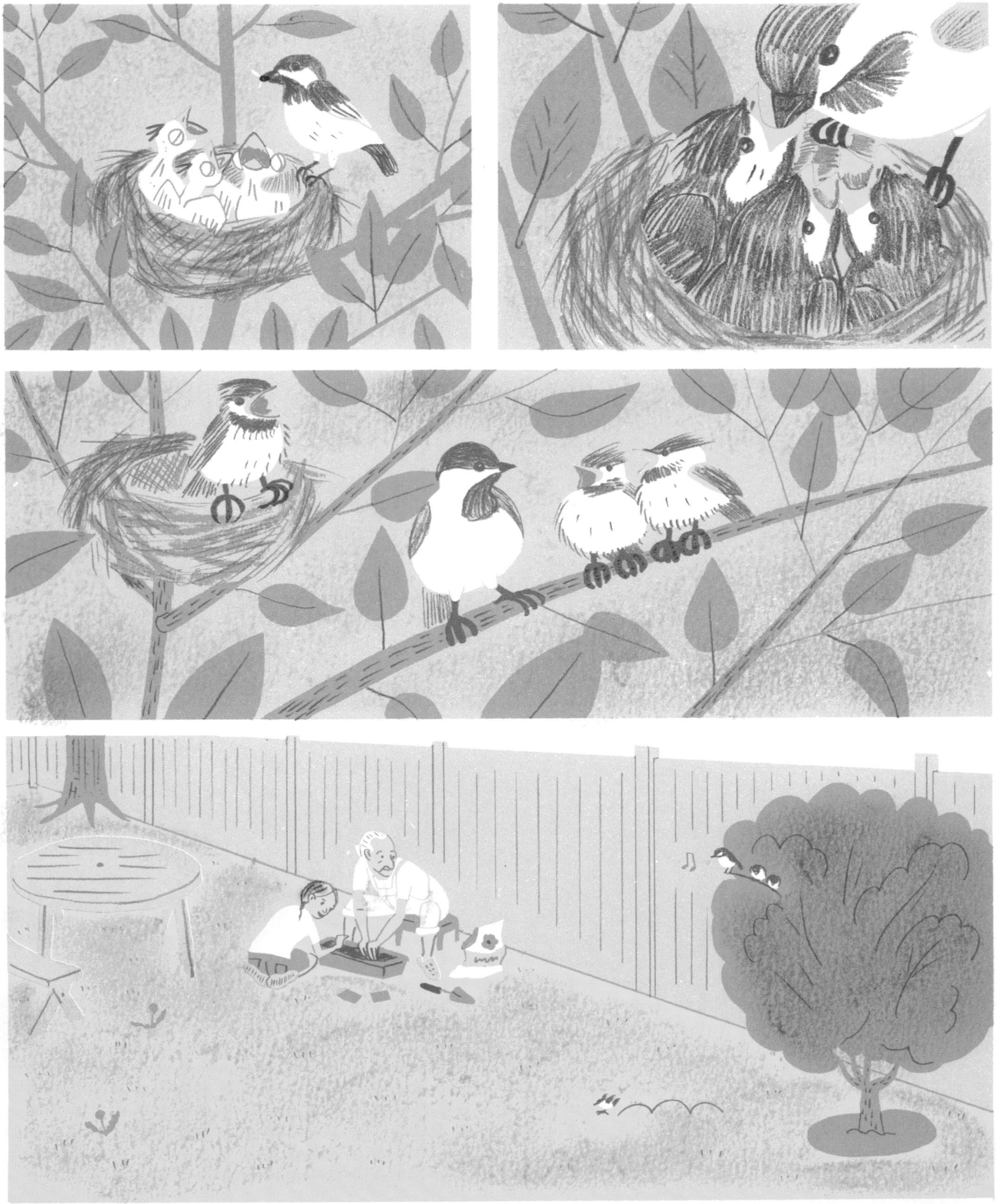

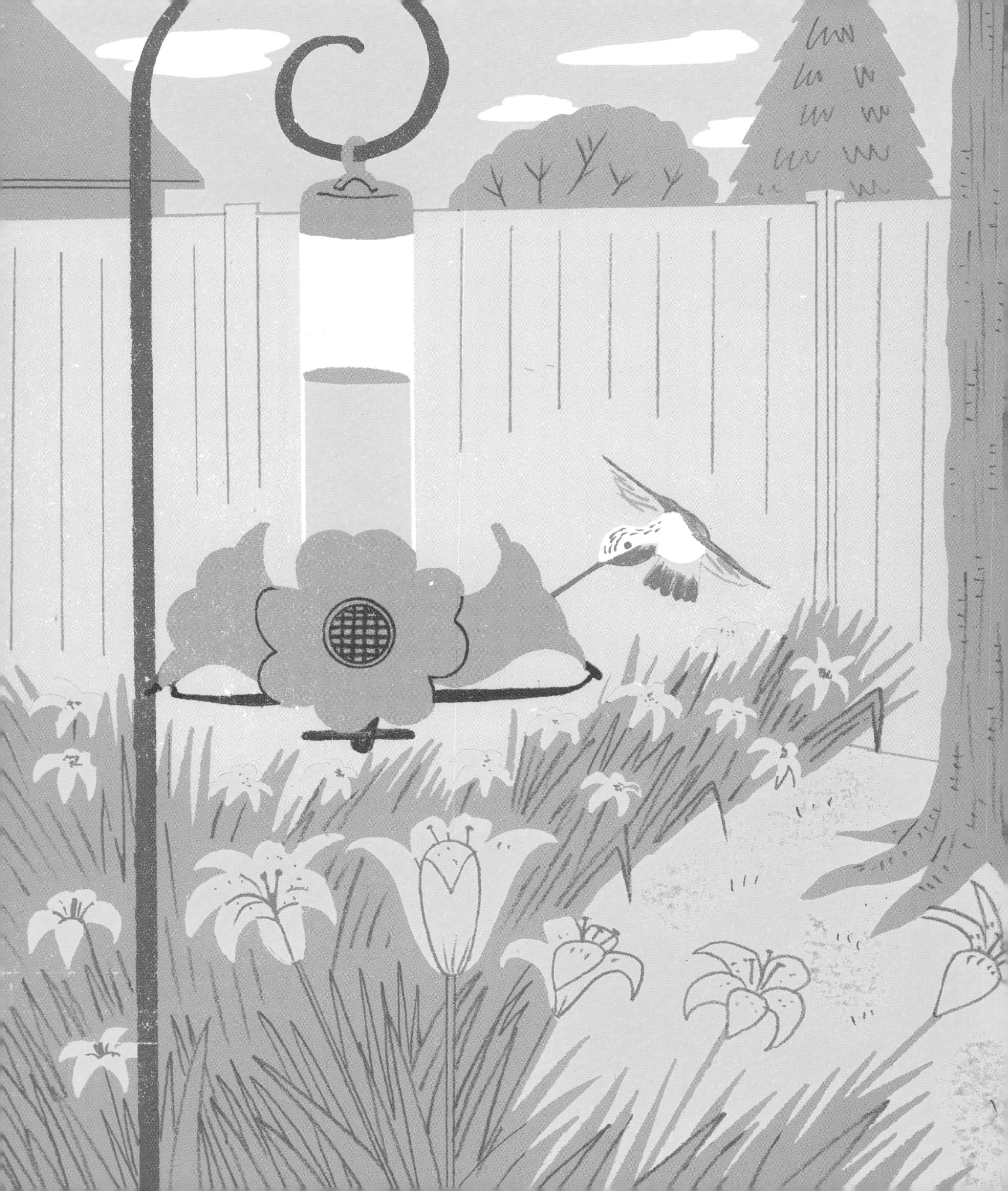

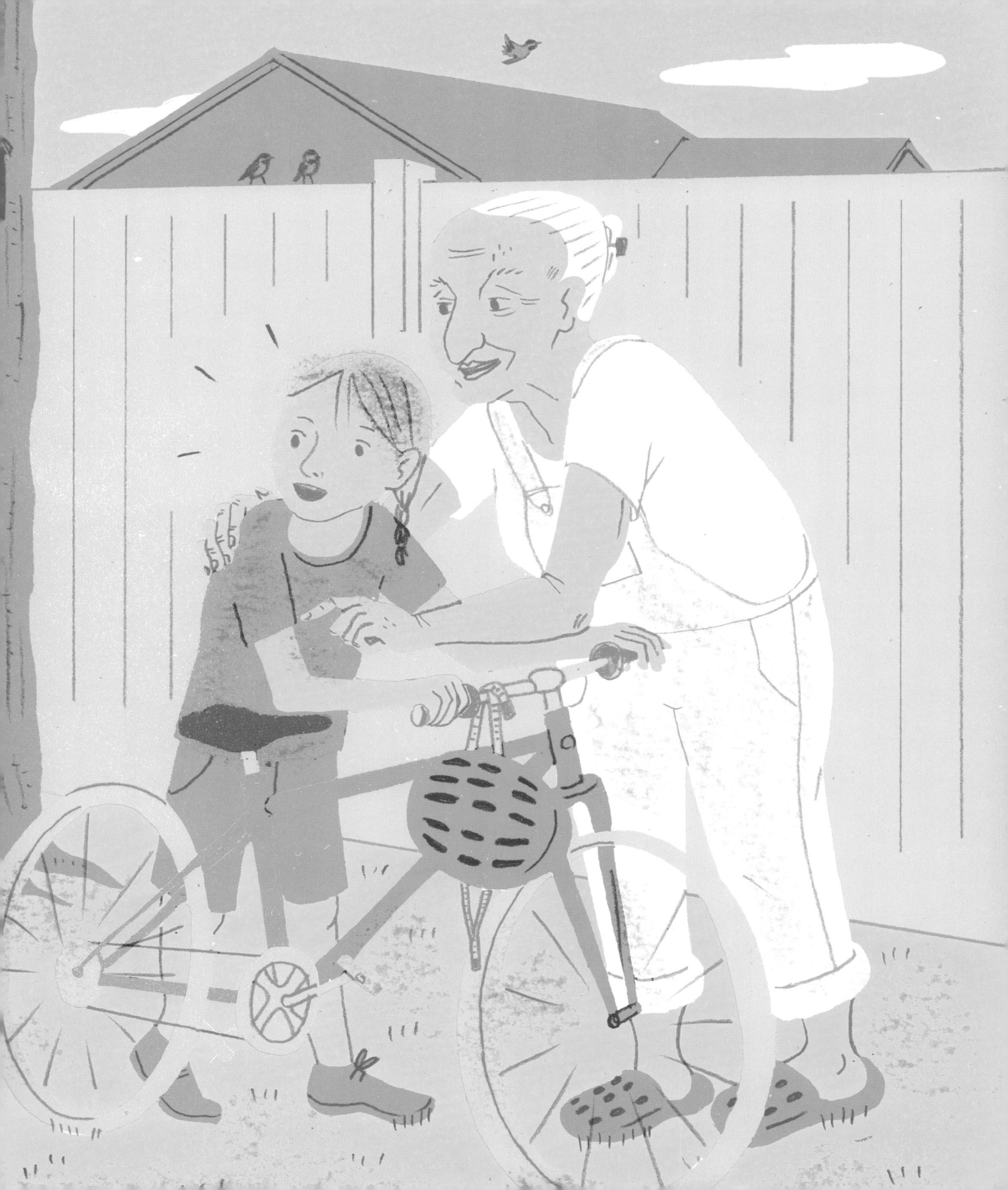

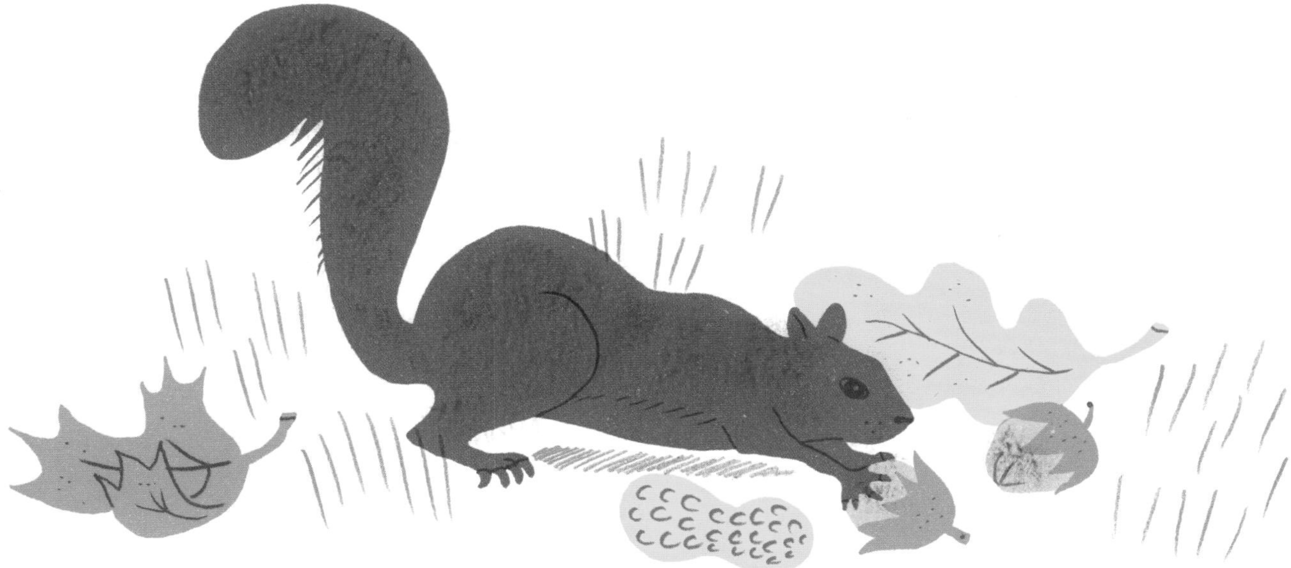

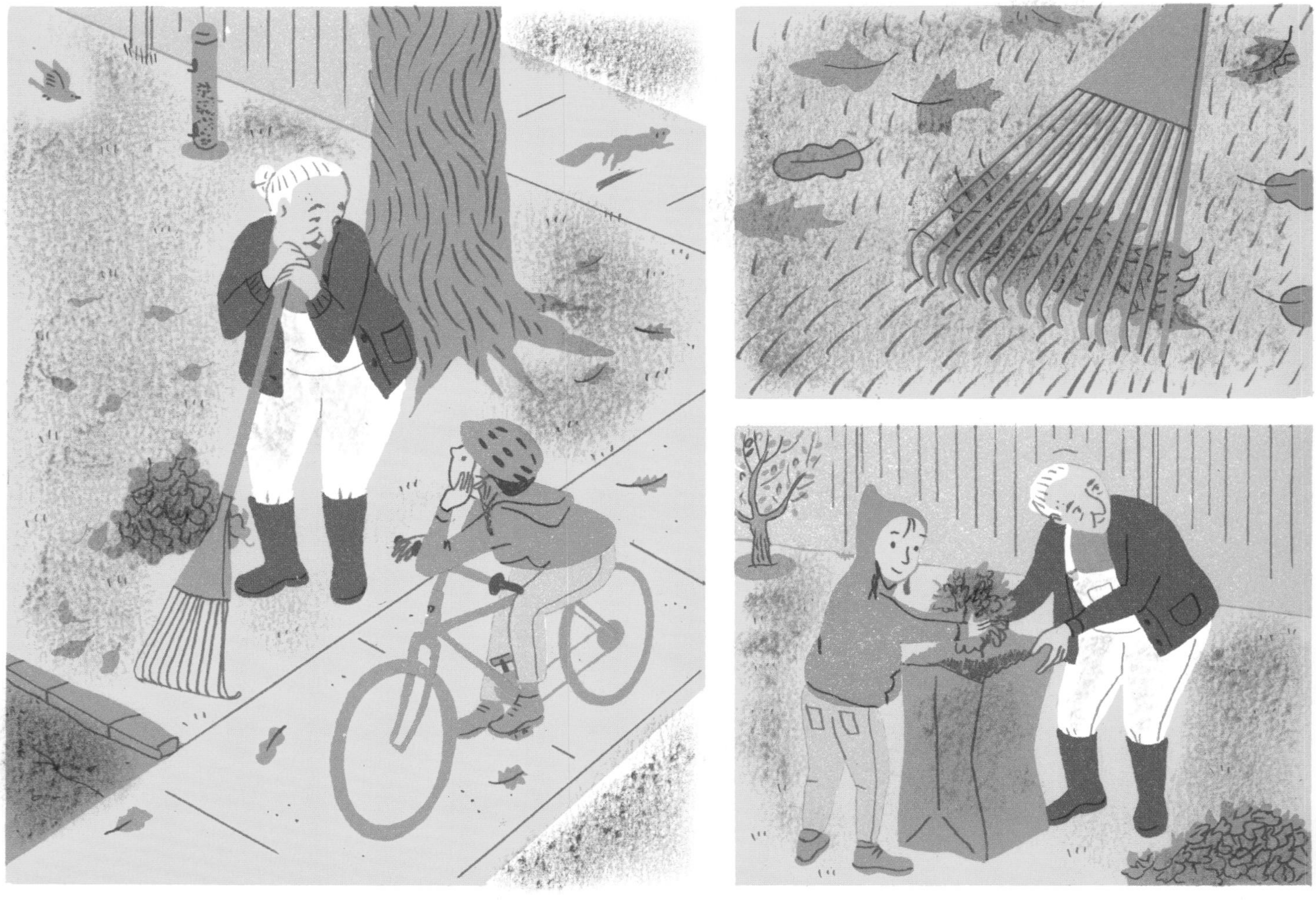

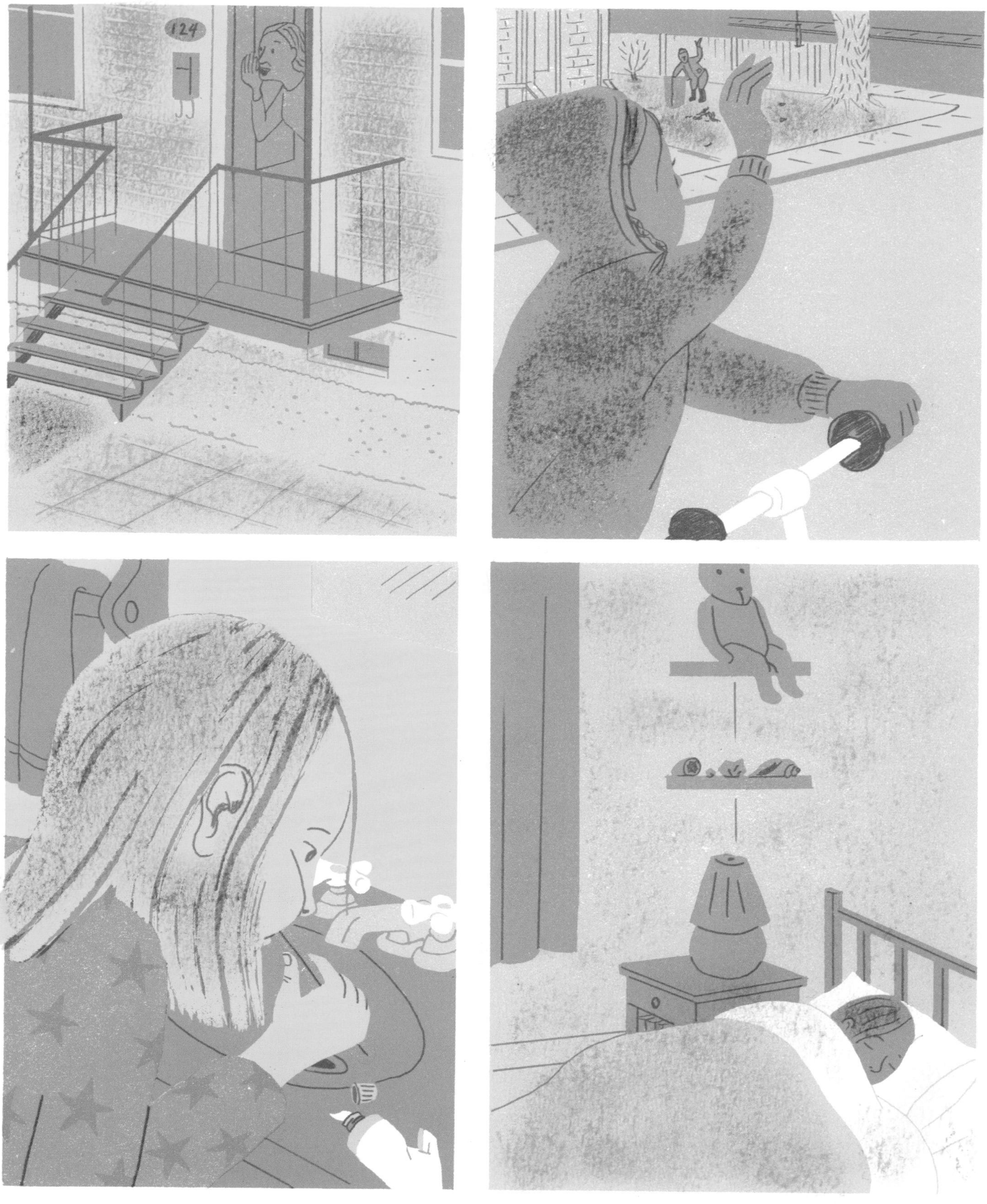
124

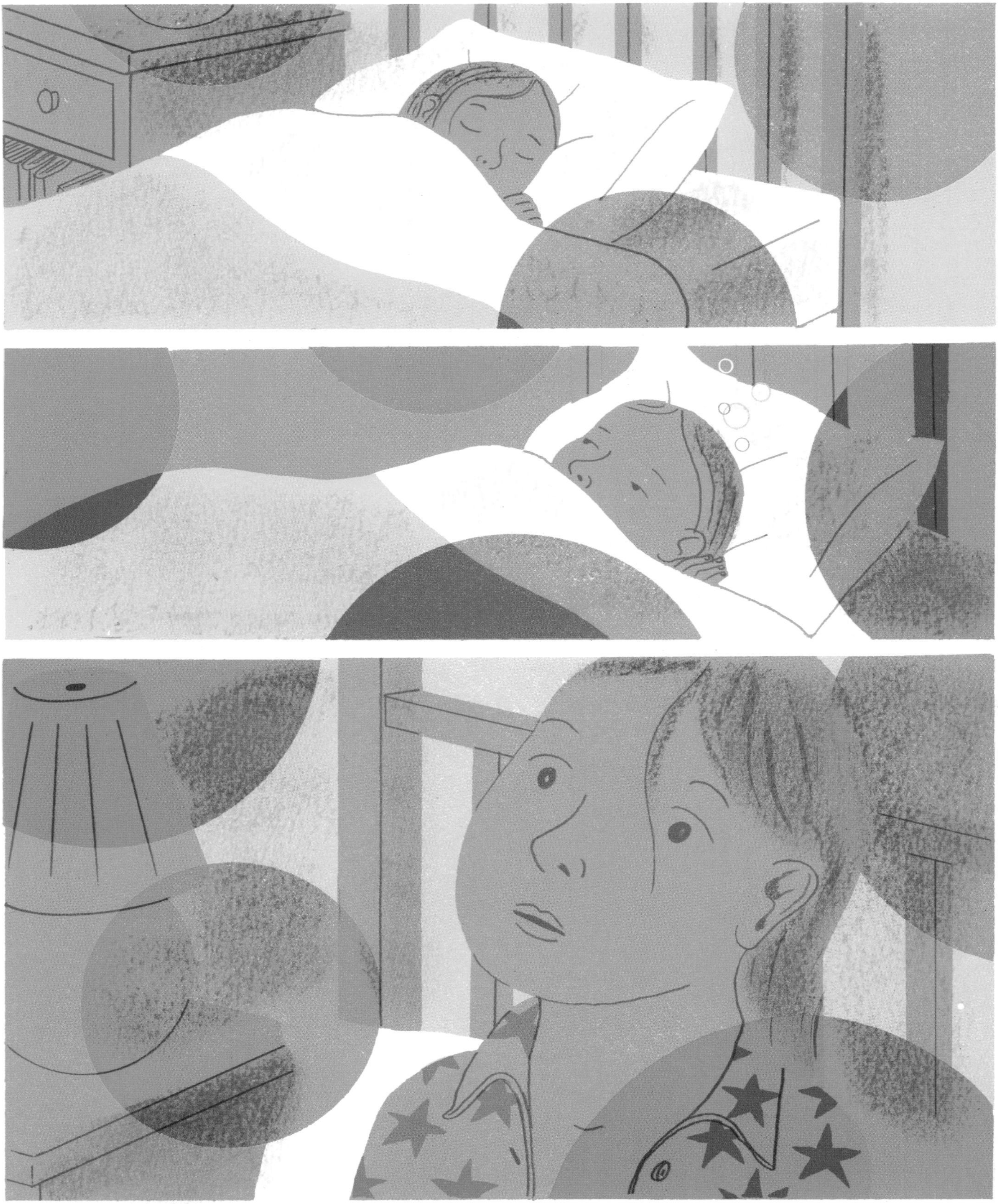

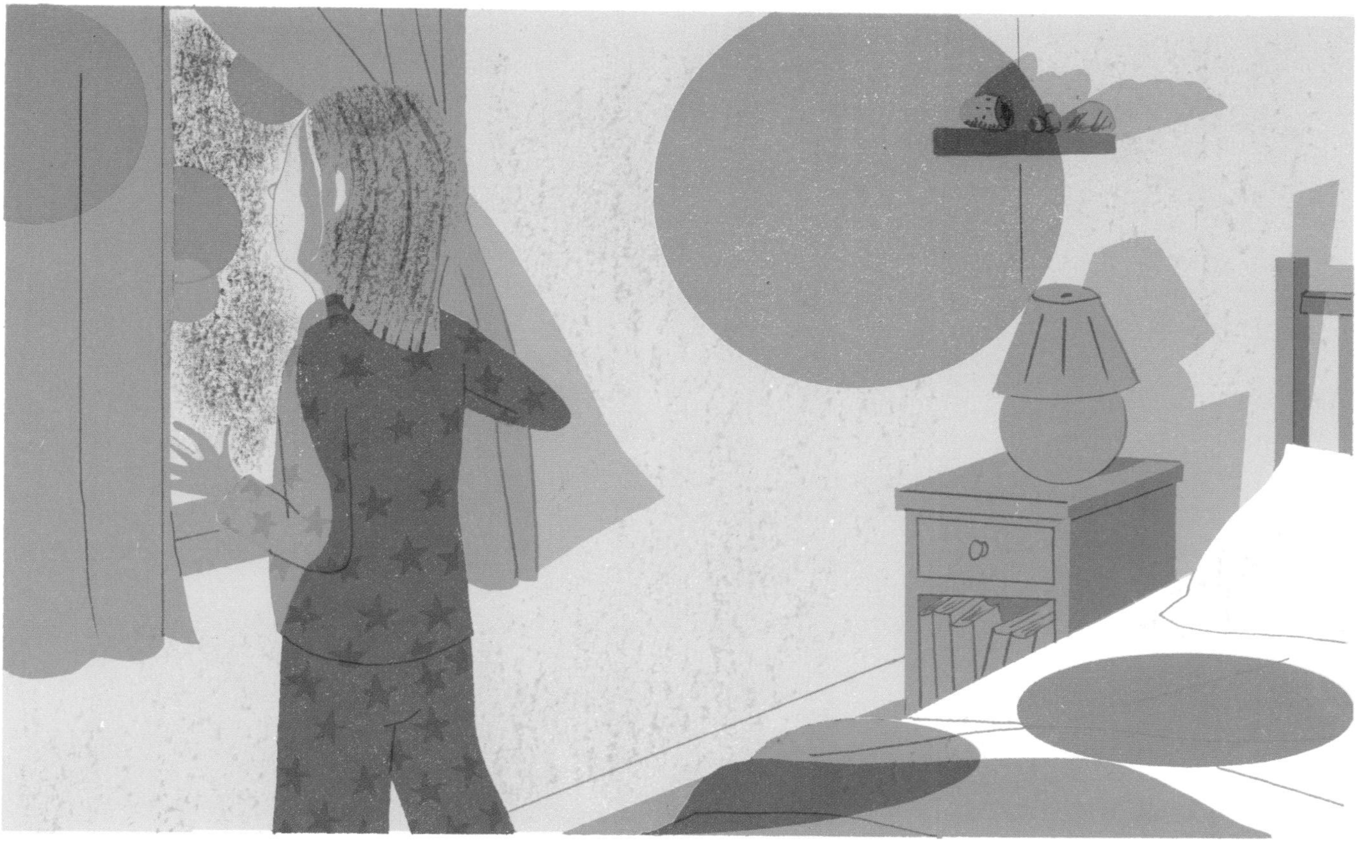
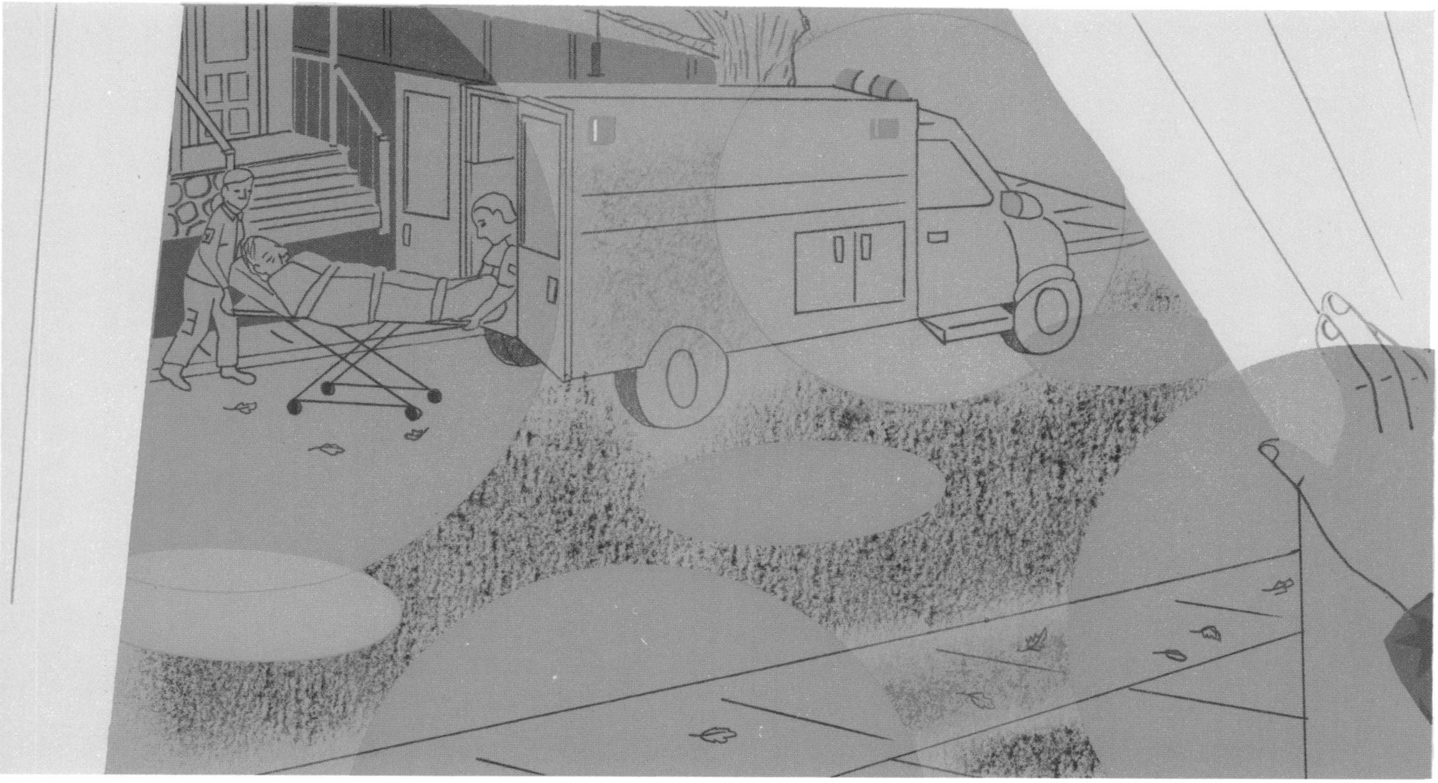

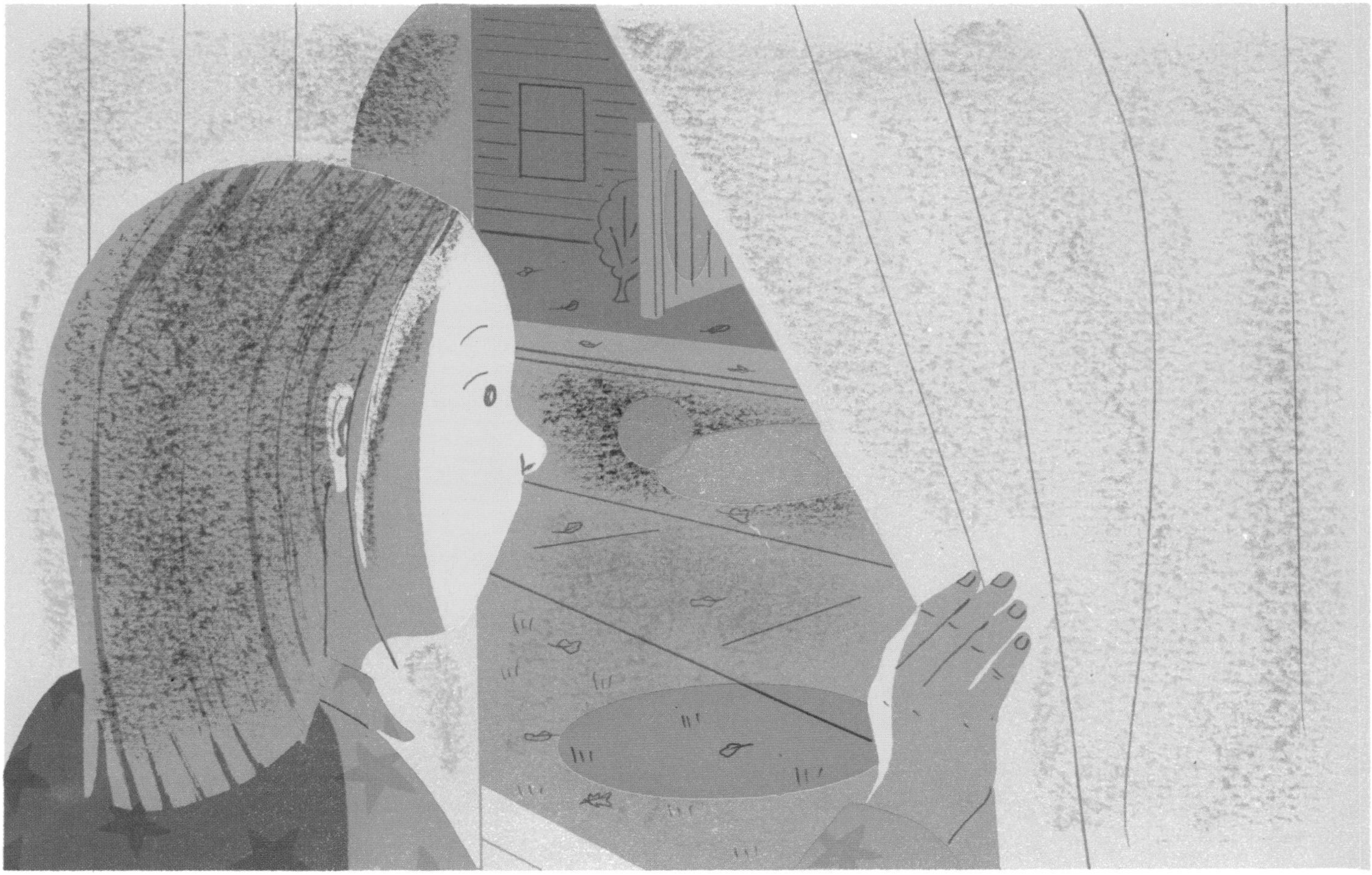

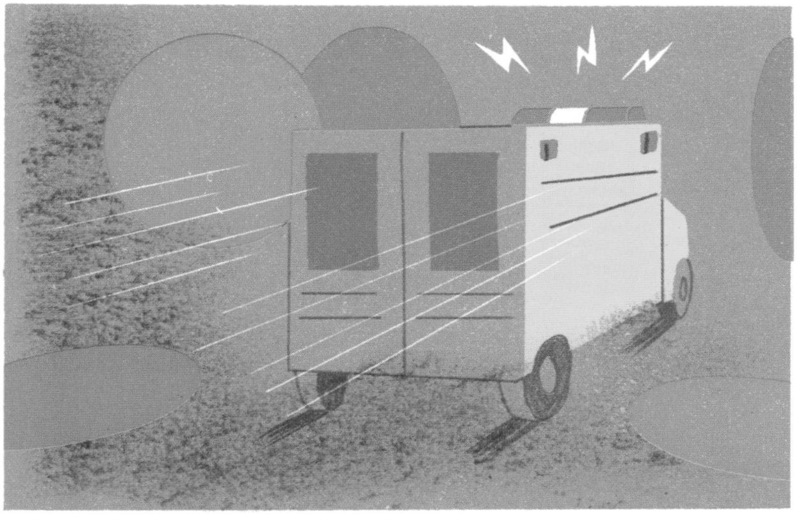

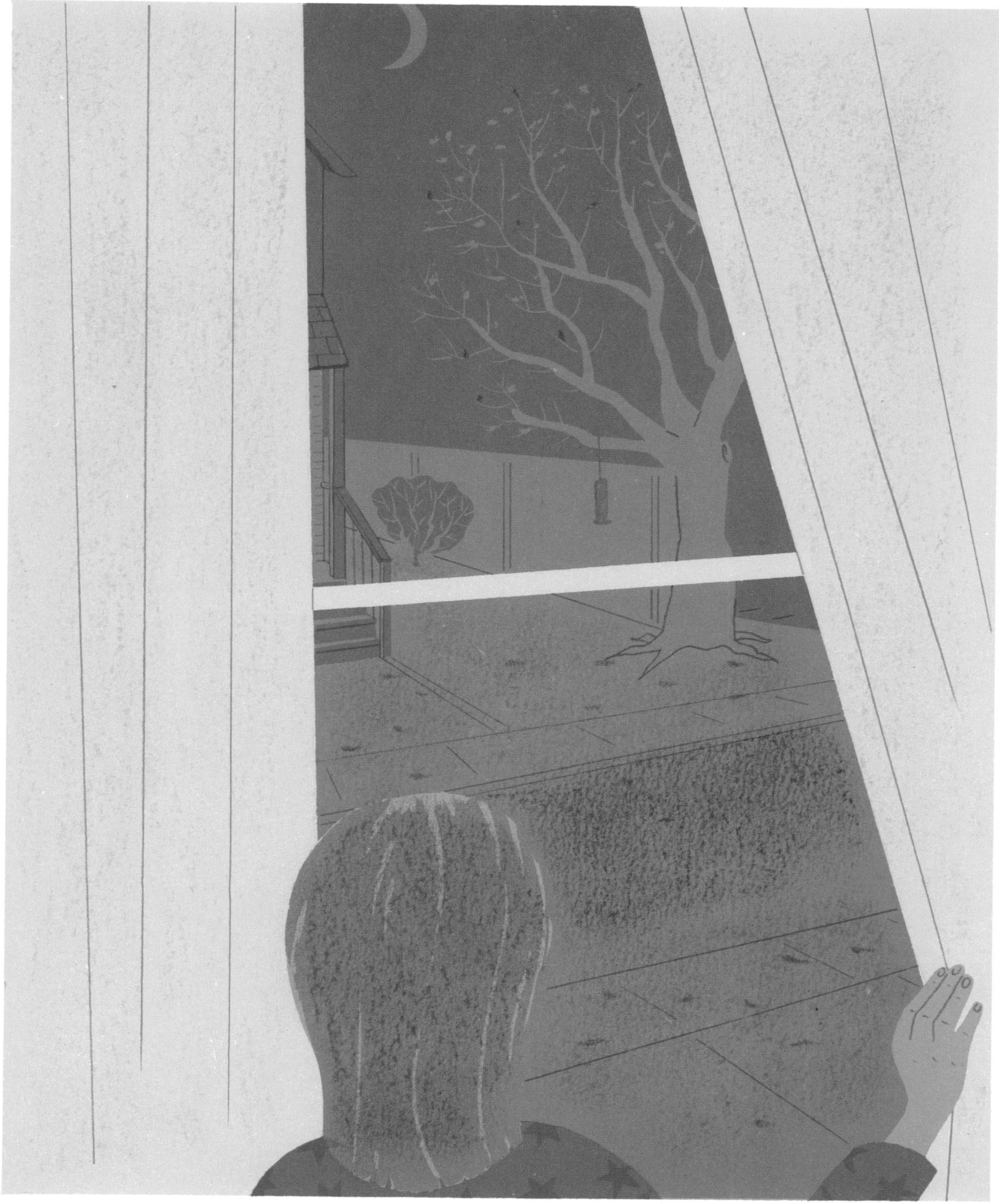

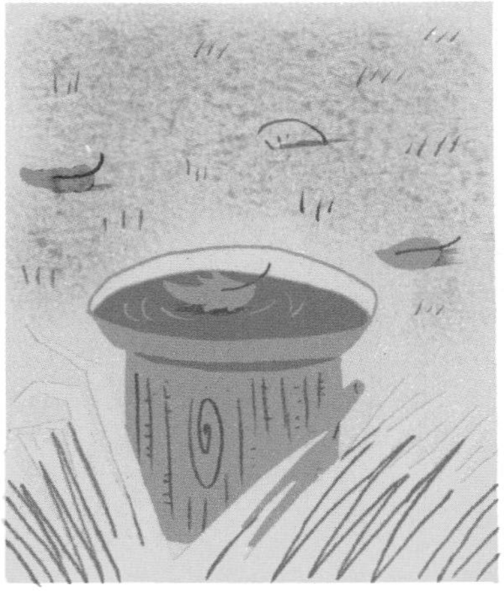

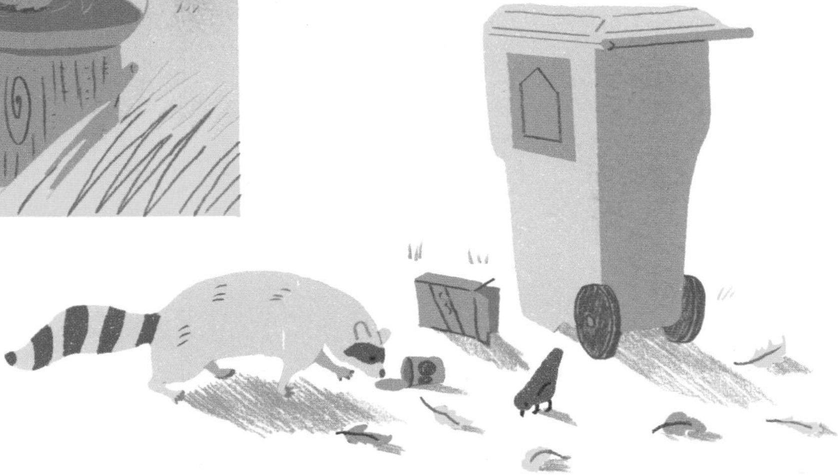

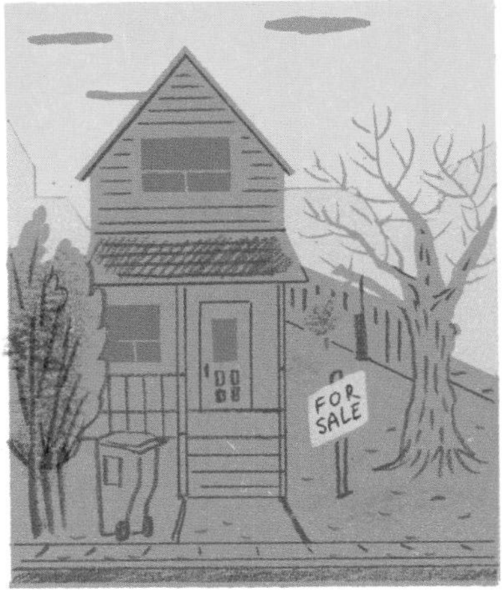
FOR SALE

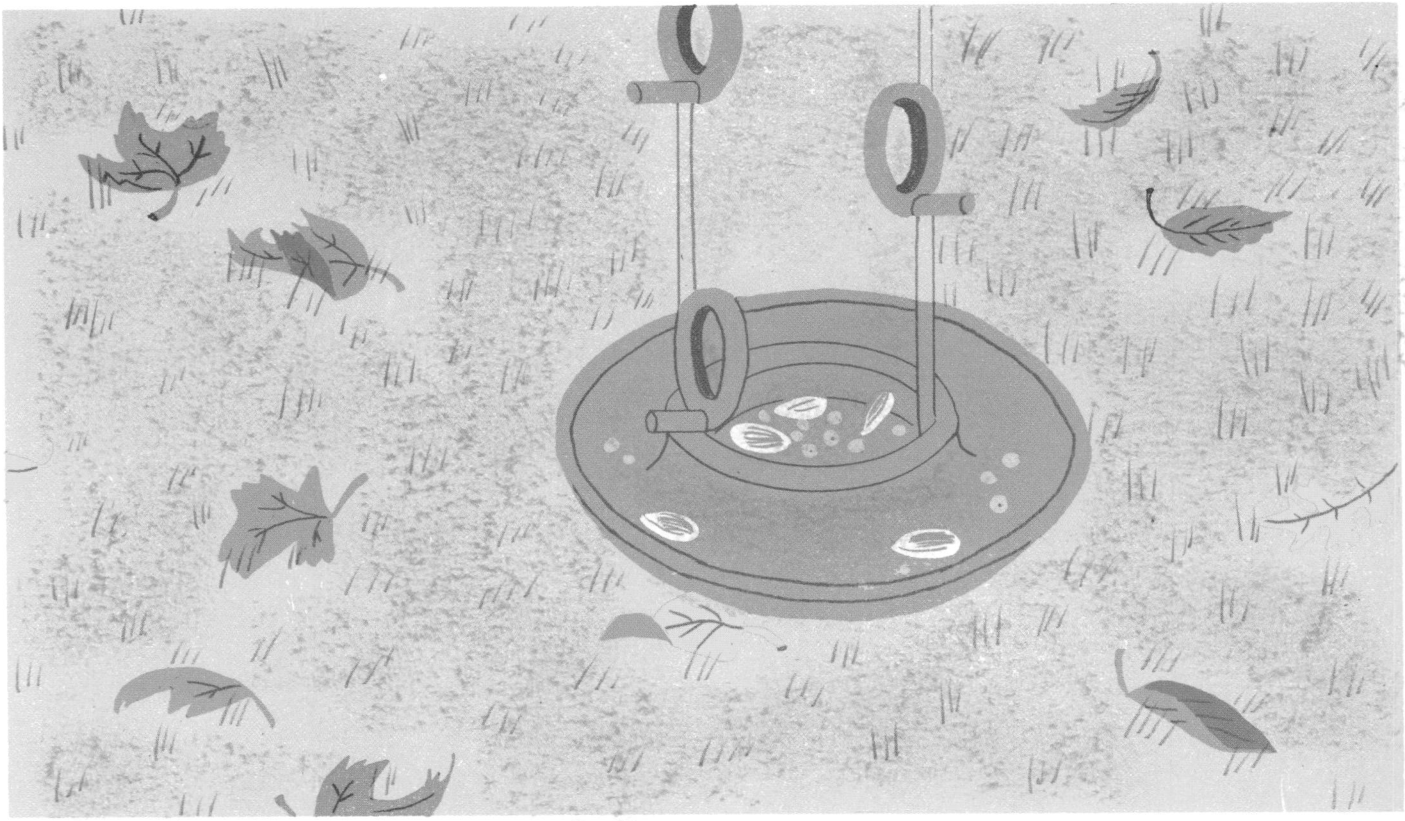

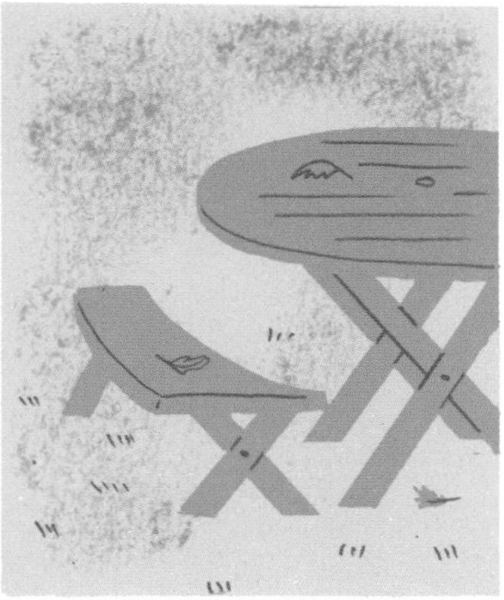

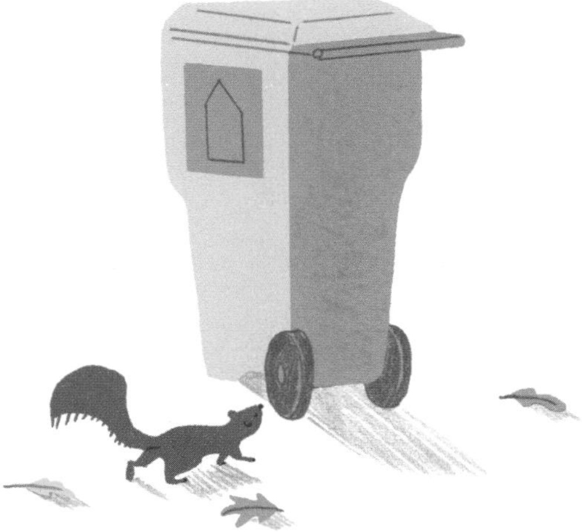

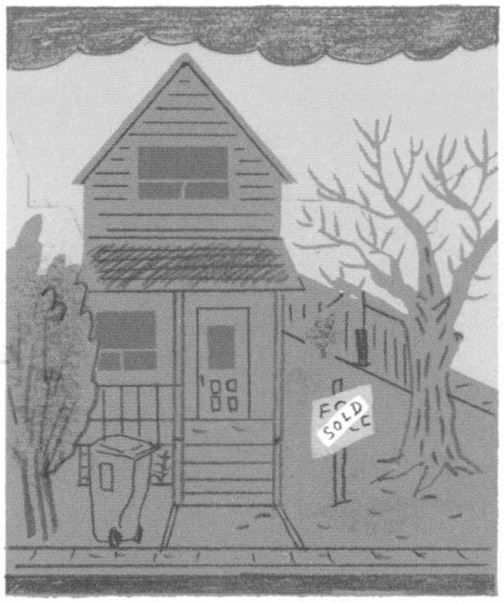
SOLD

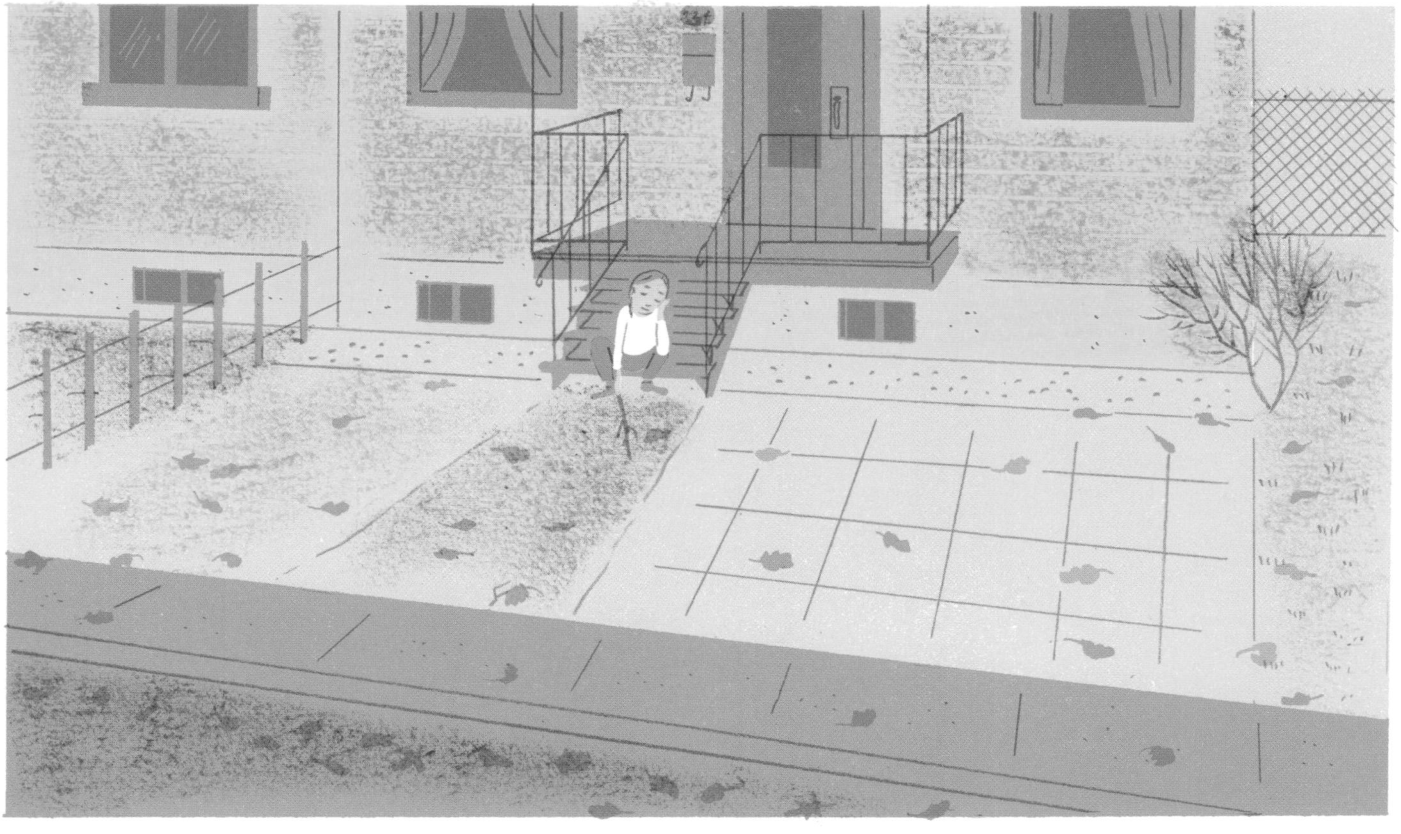

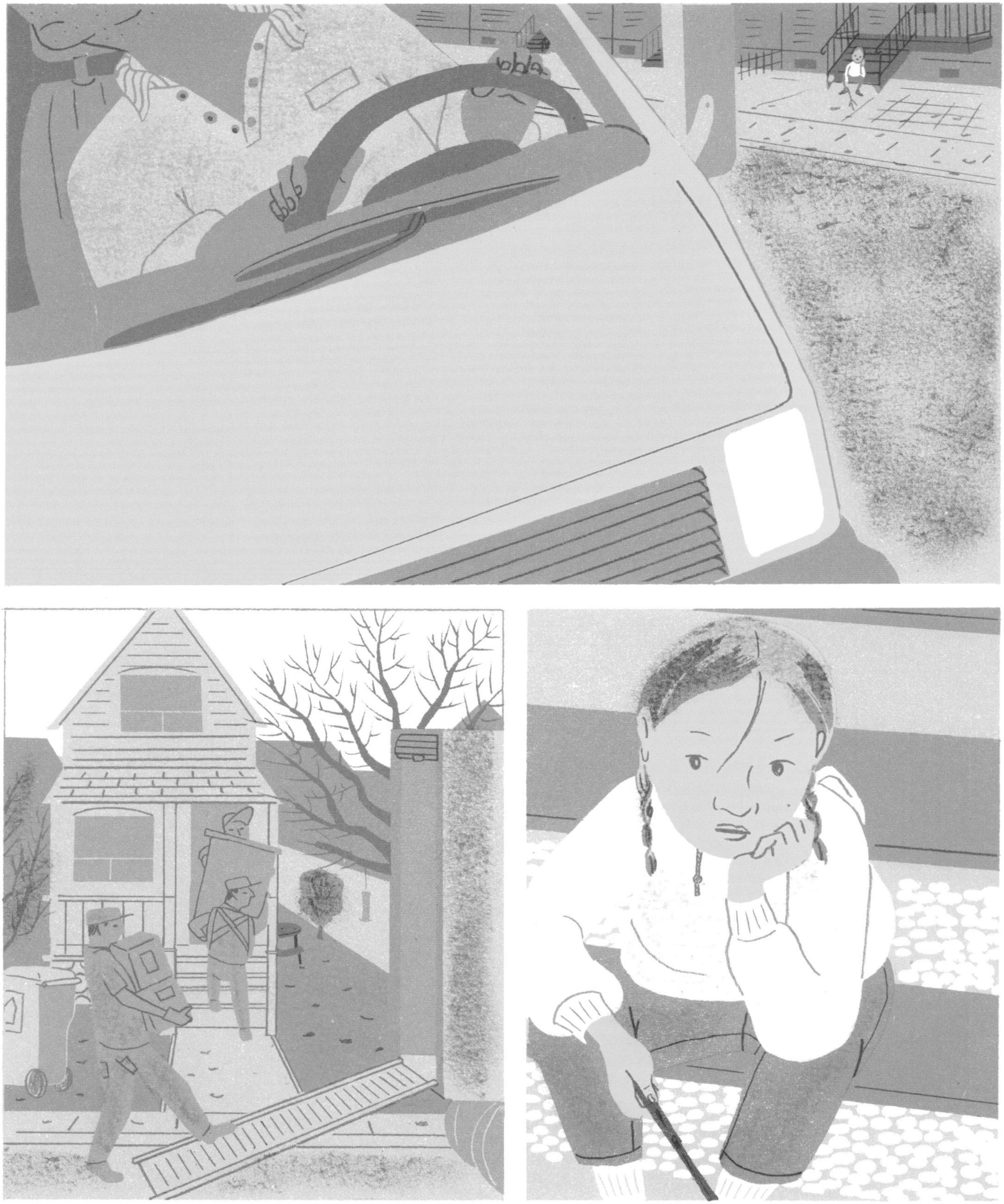

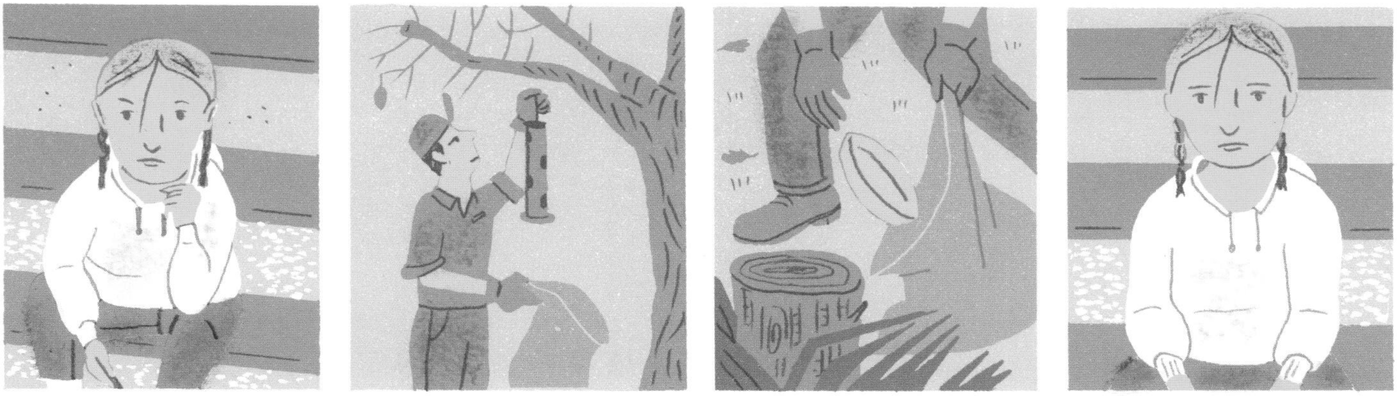

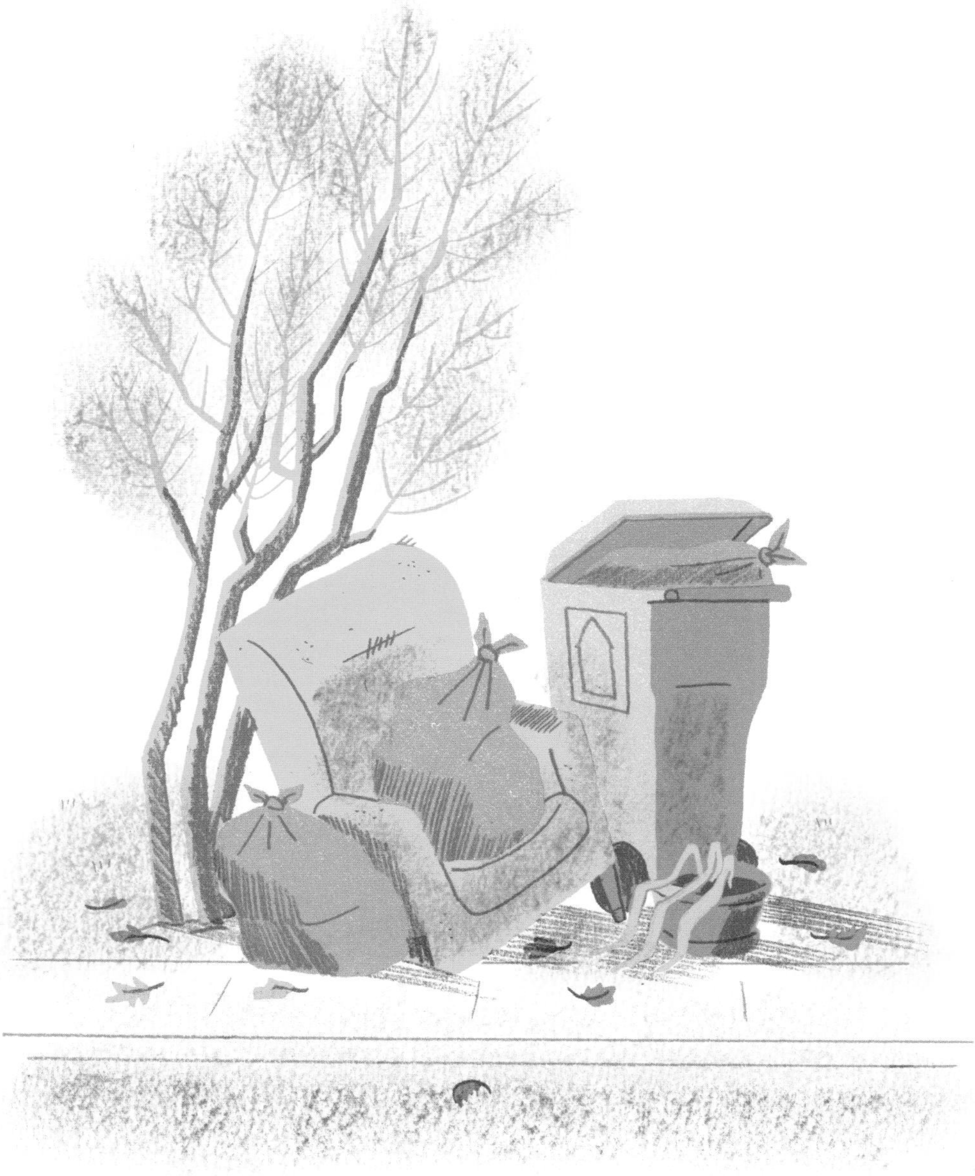

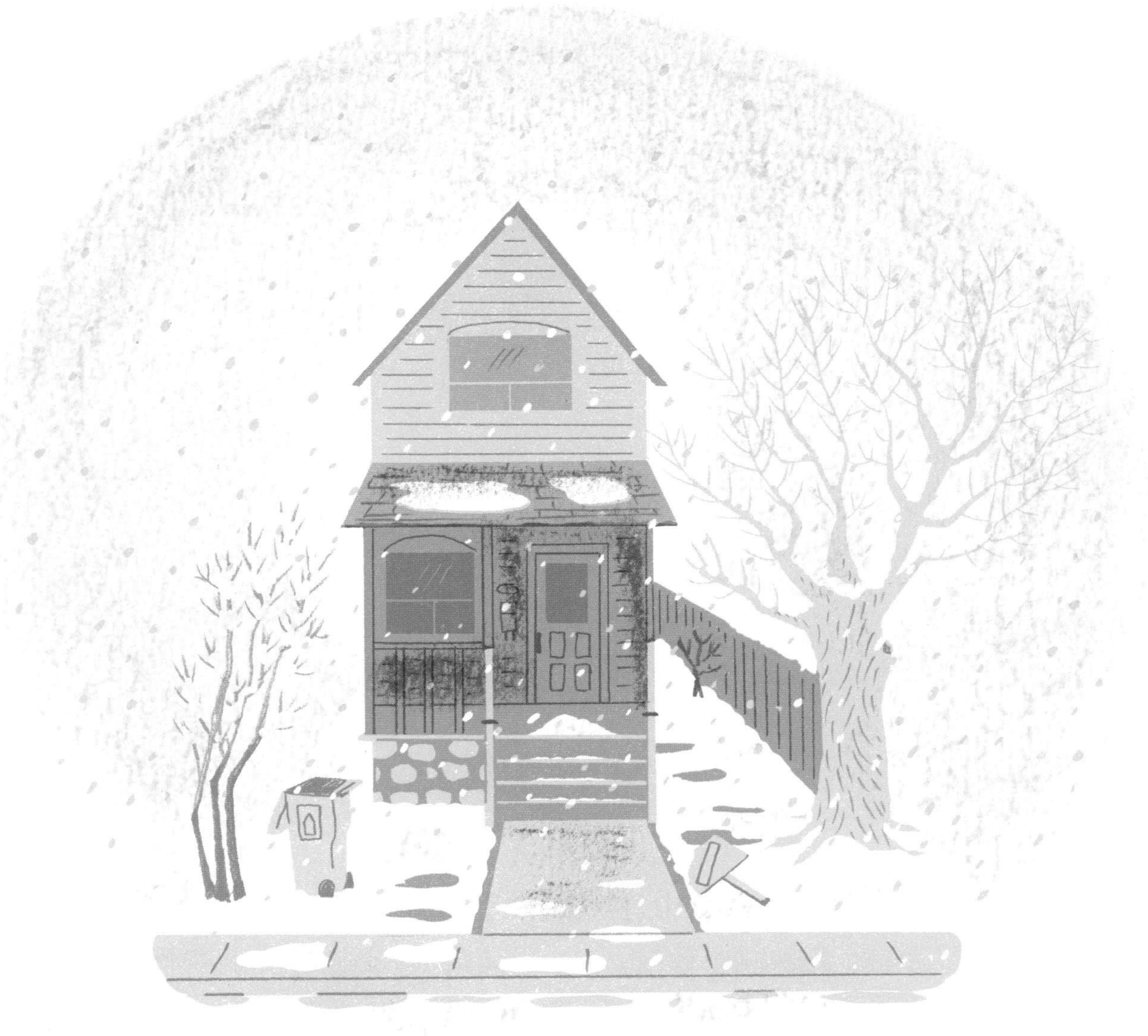

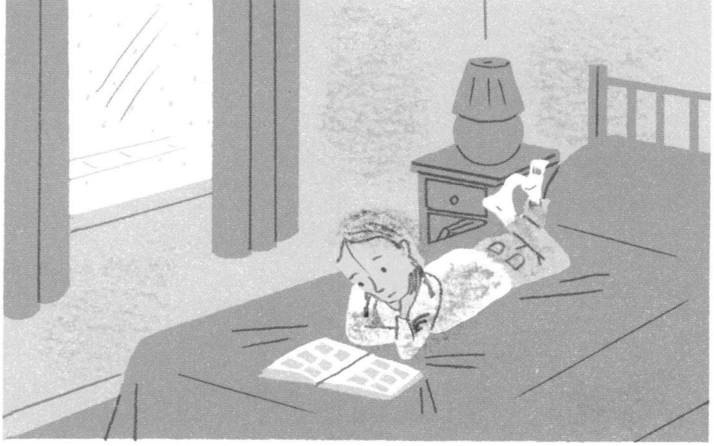

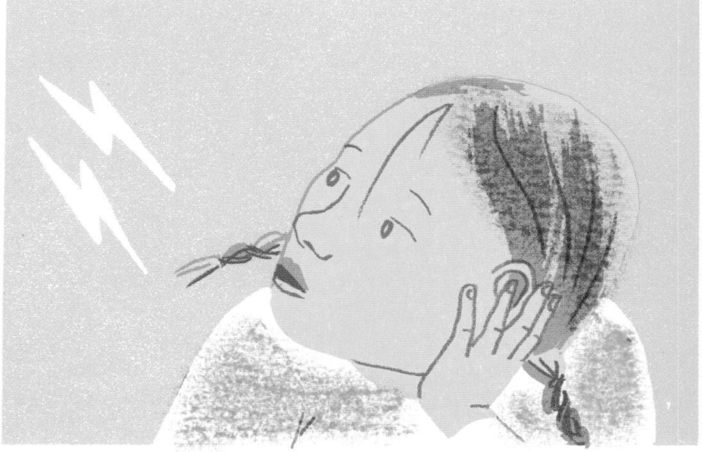

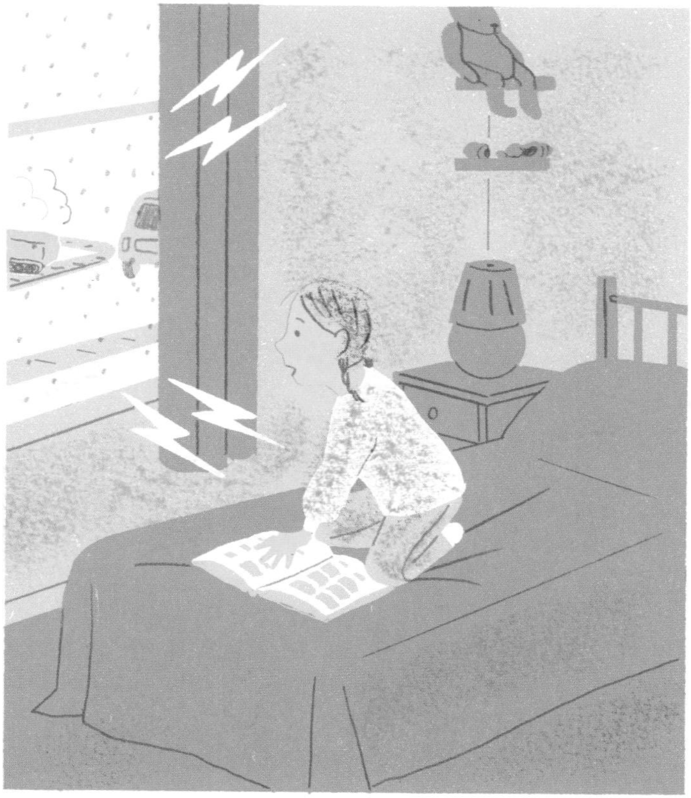
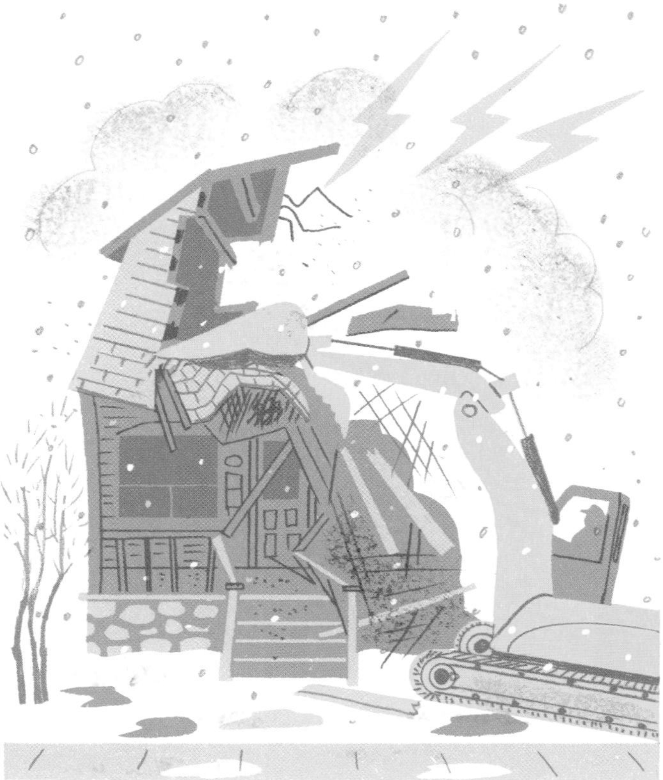
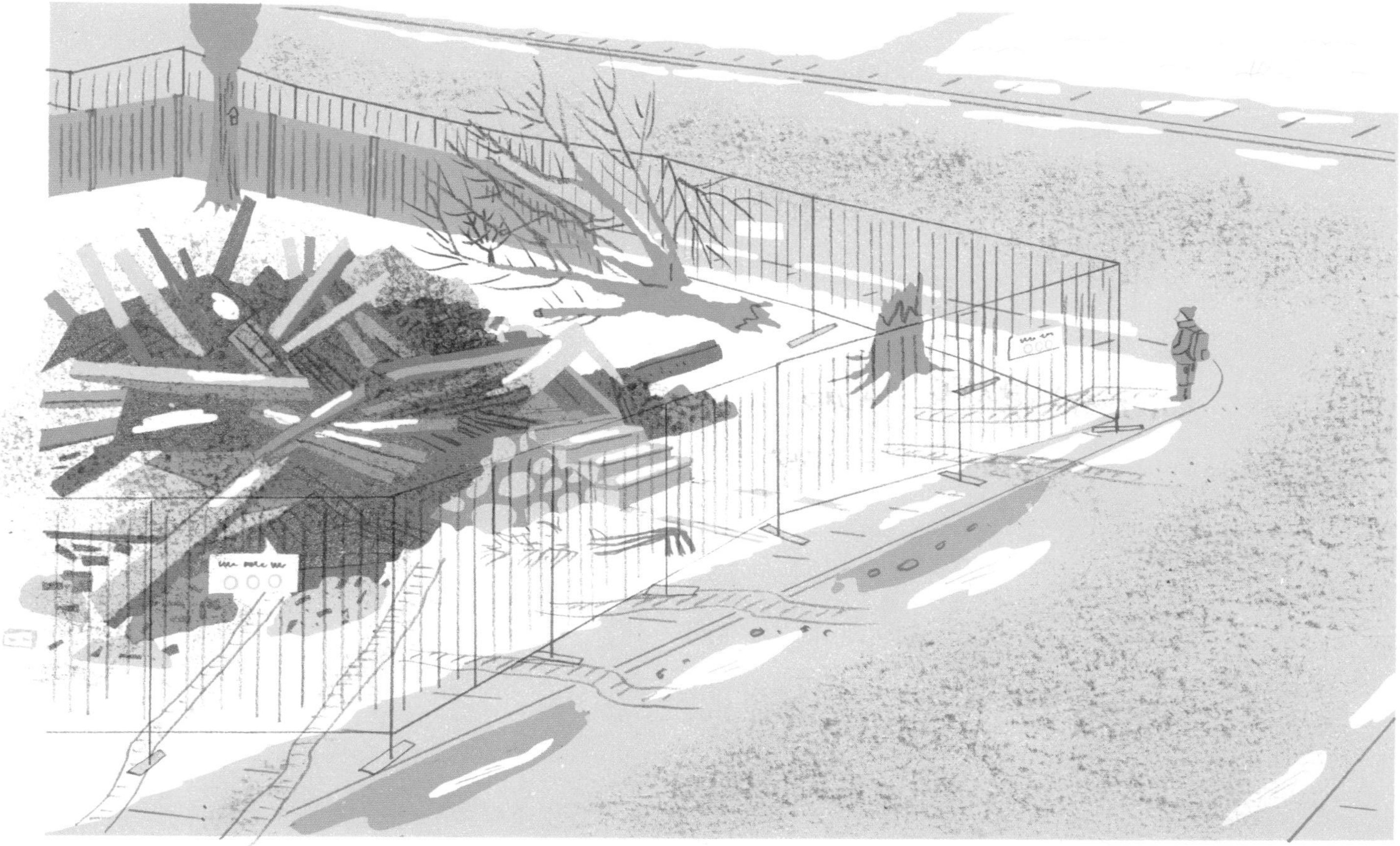

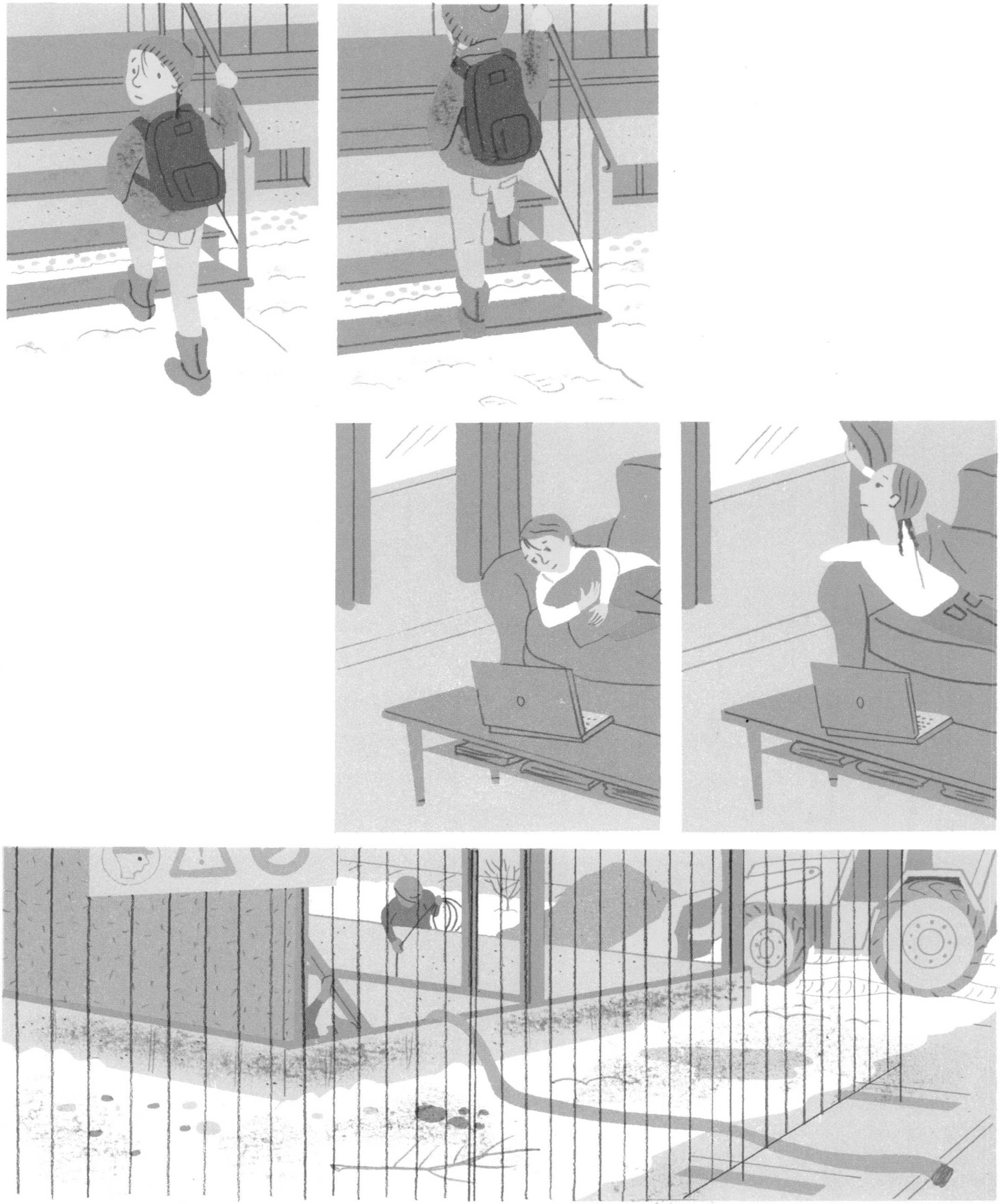

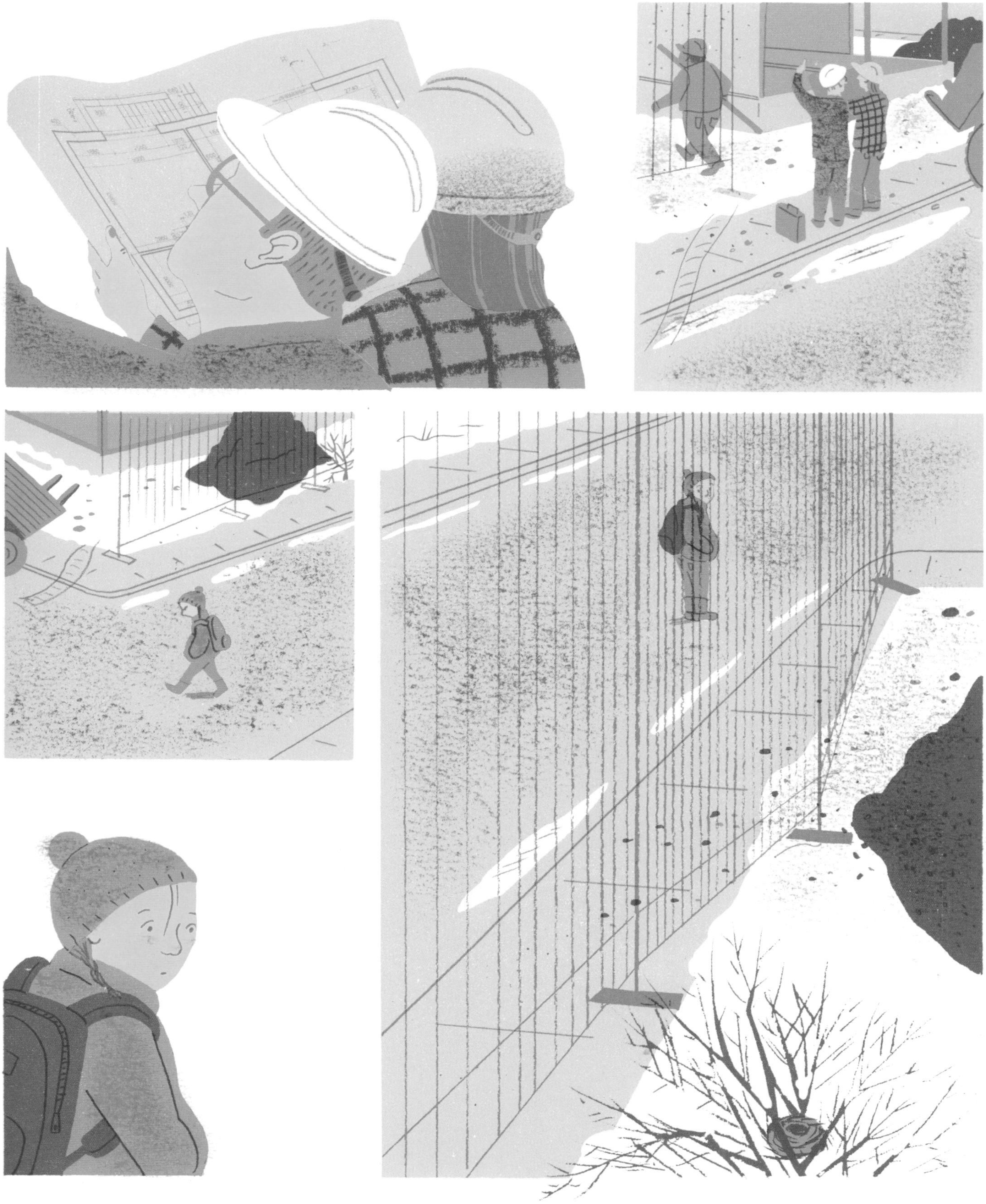

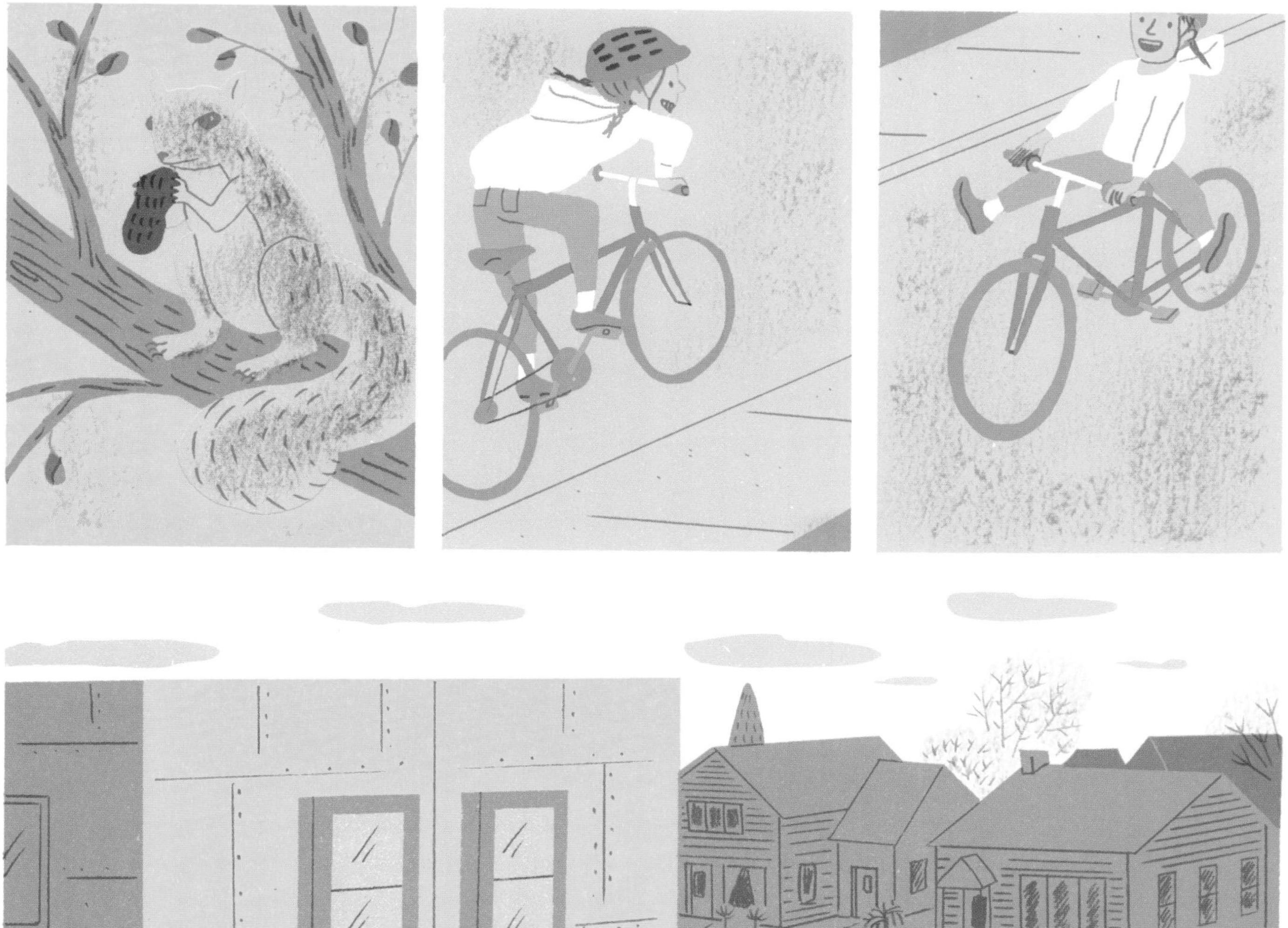

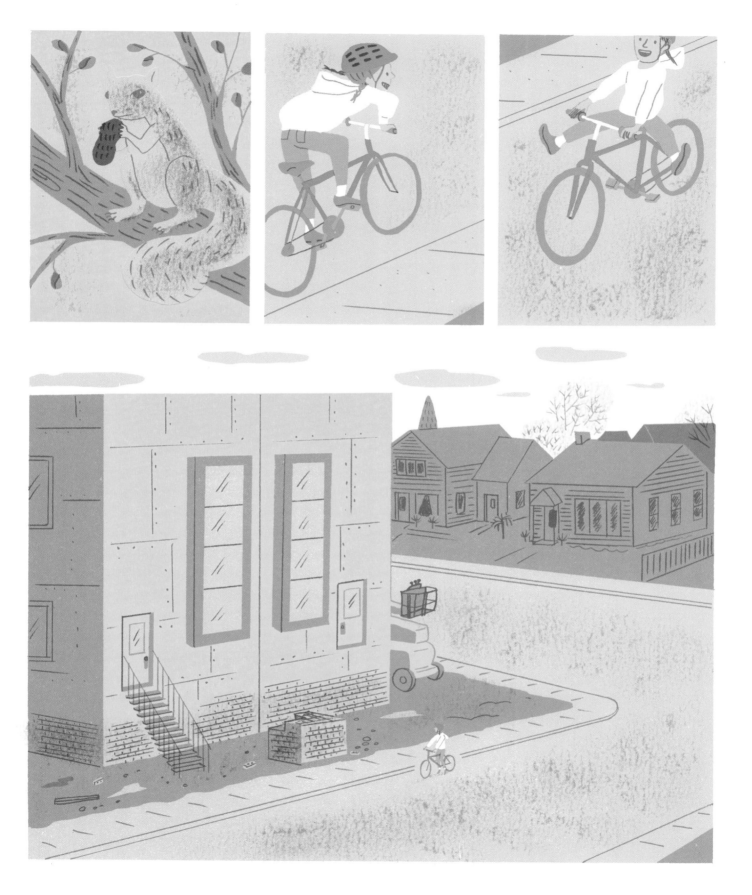

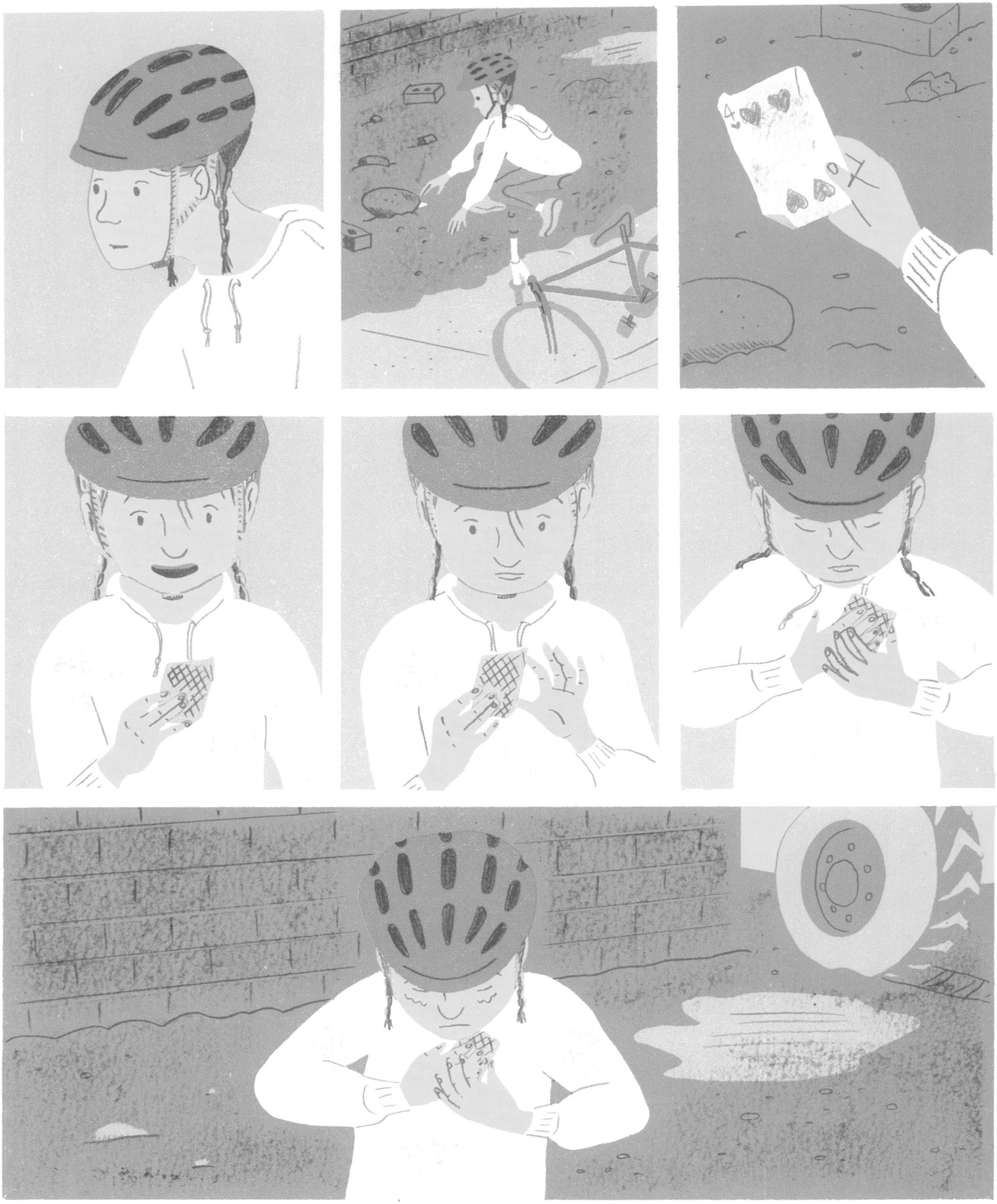

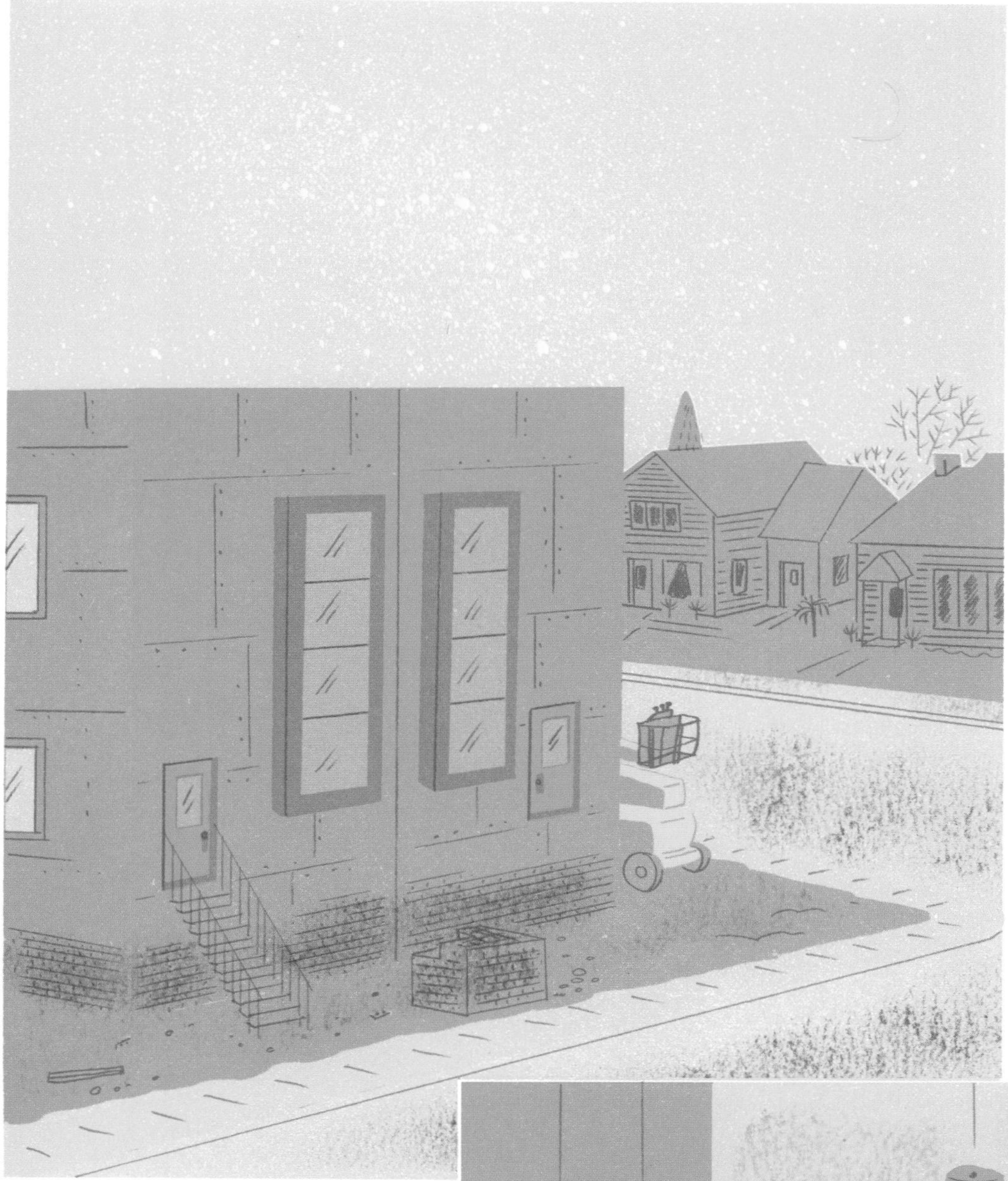

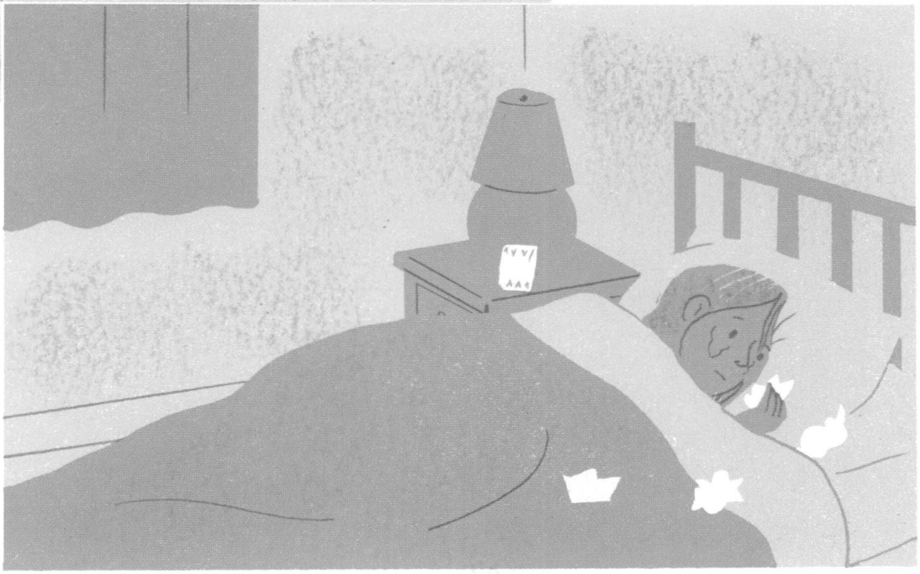

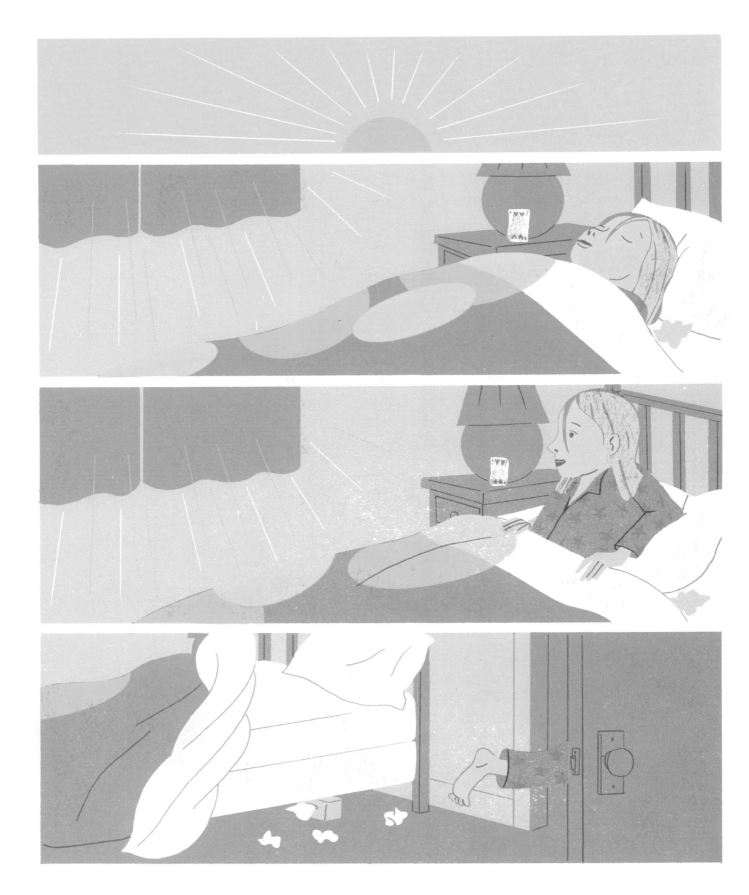

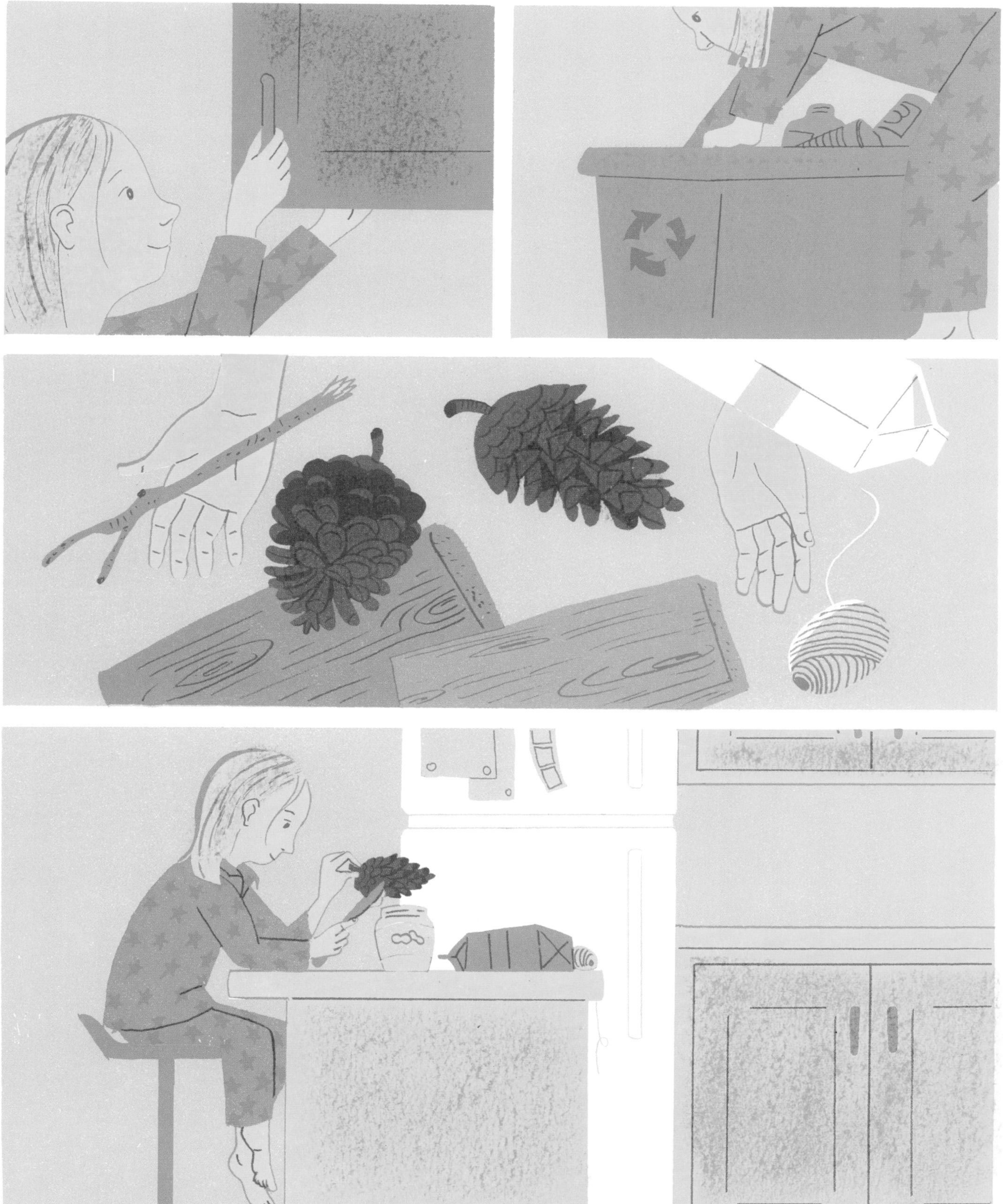

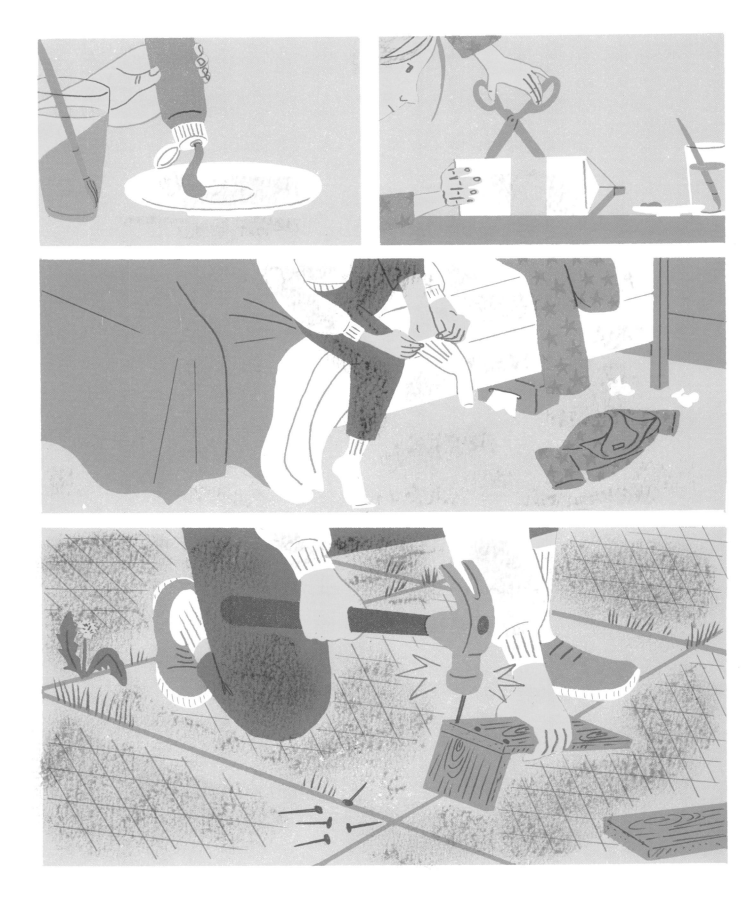

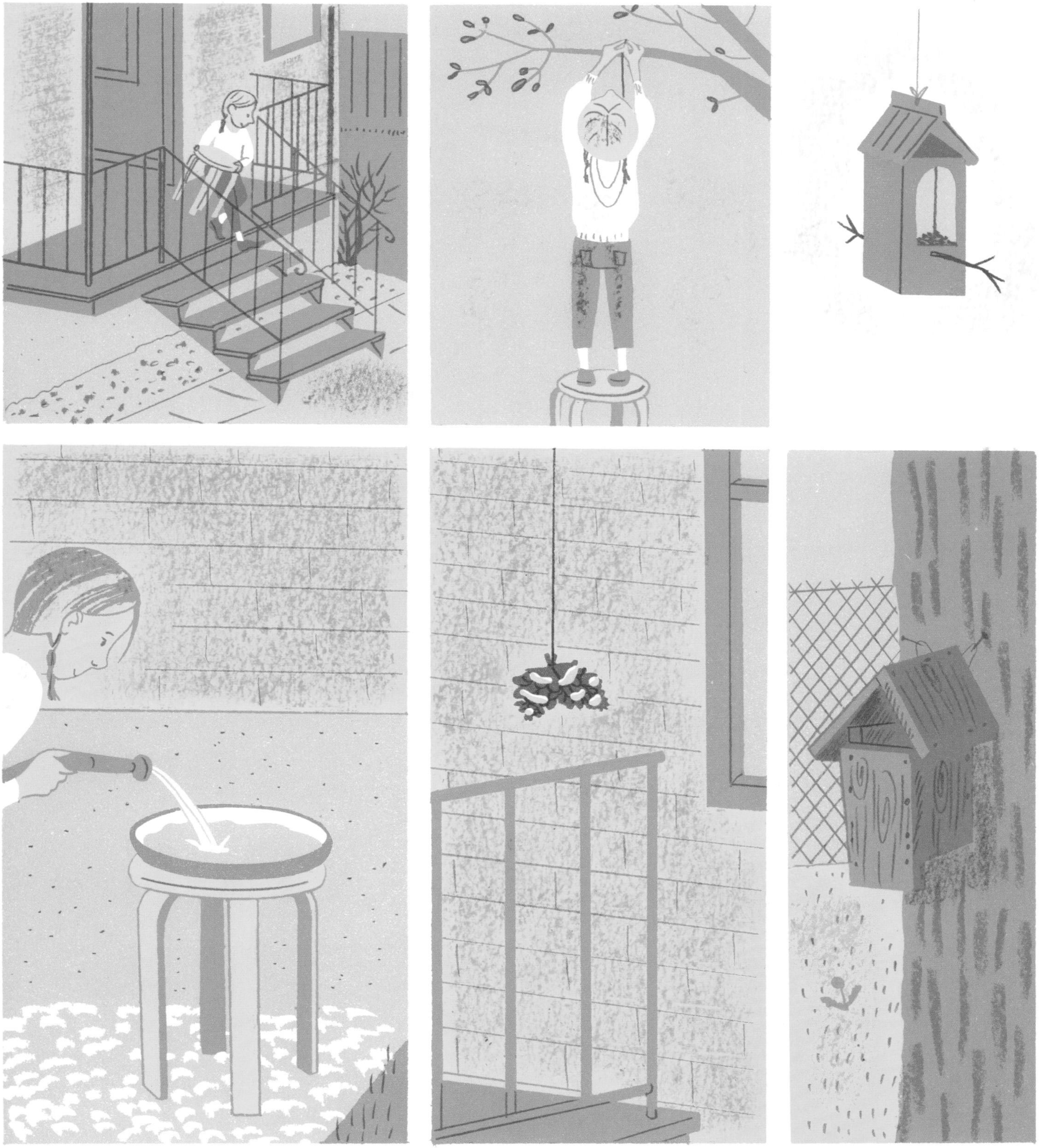

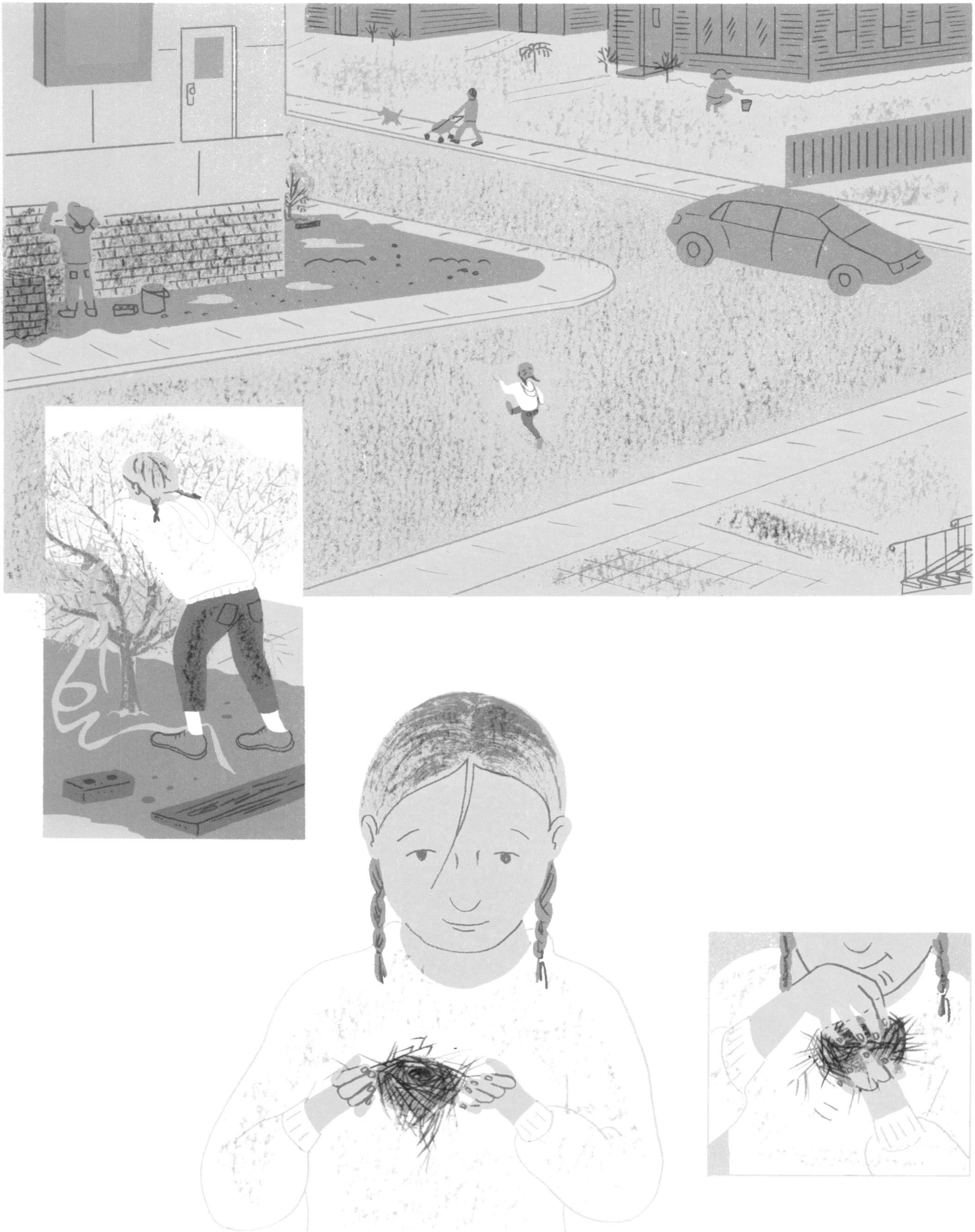

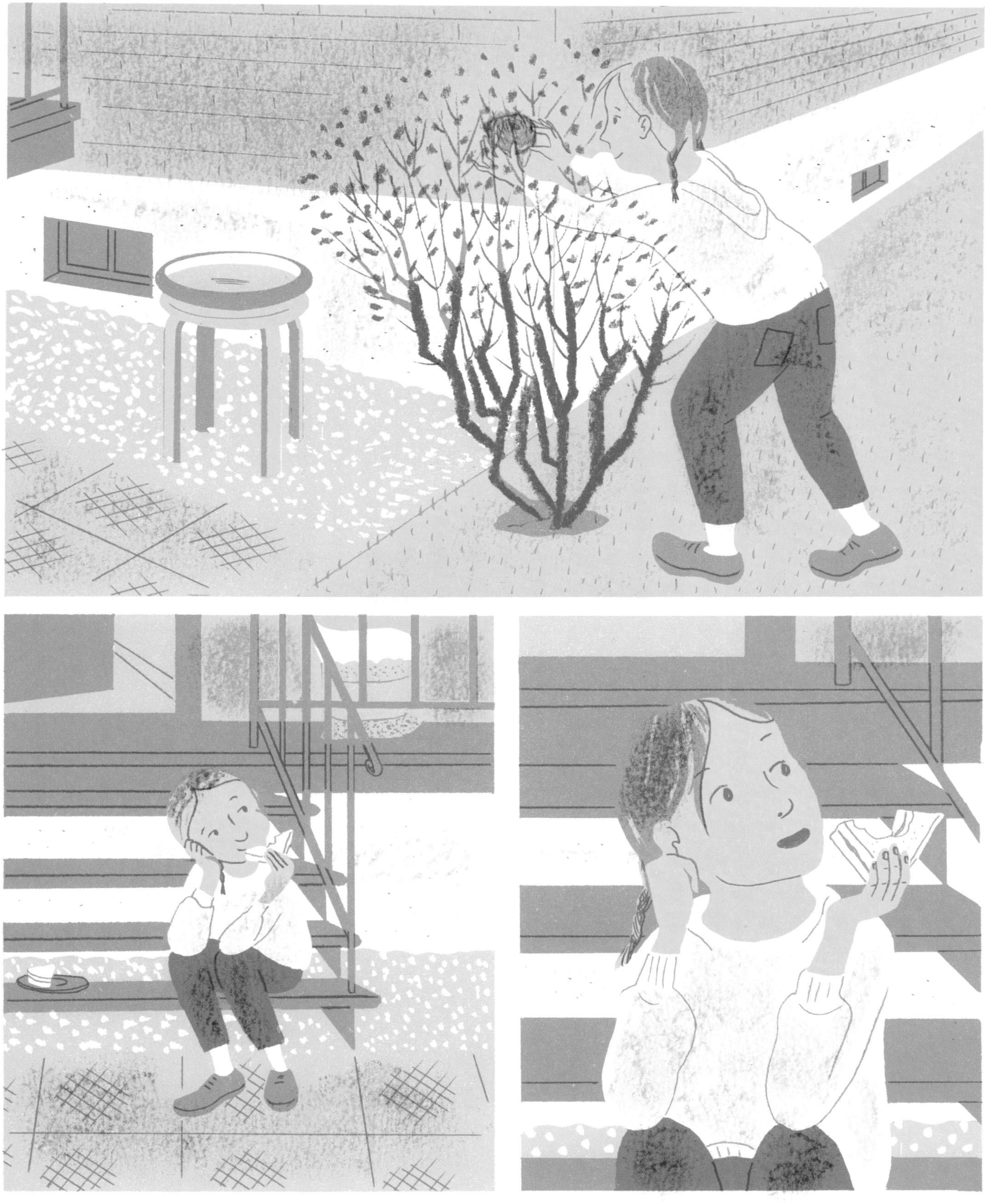

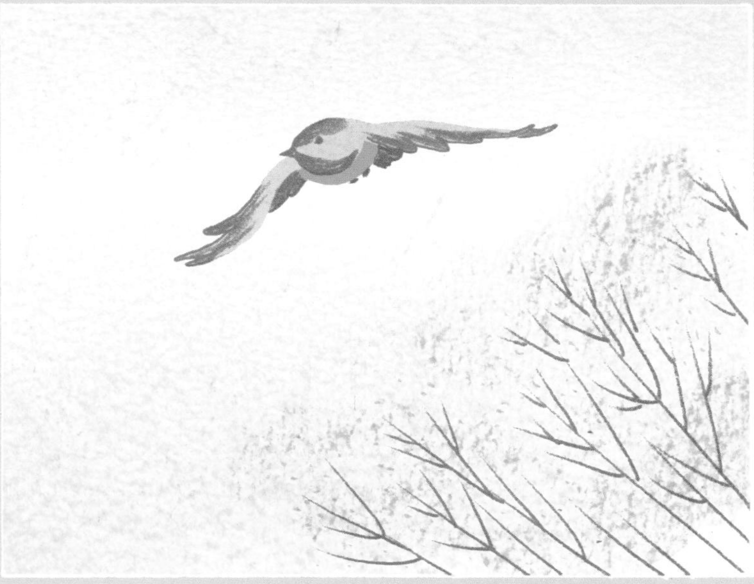
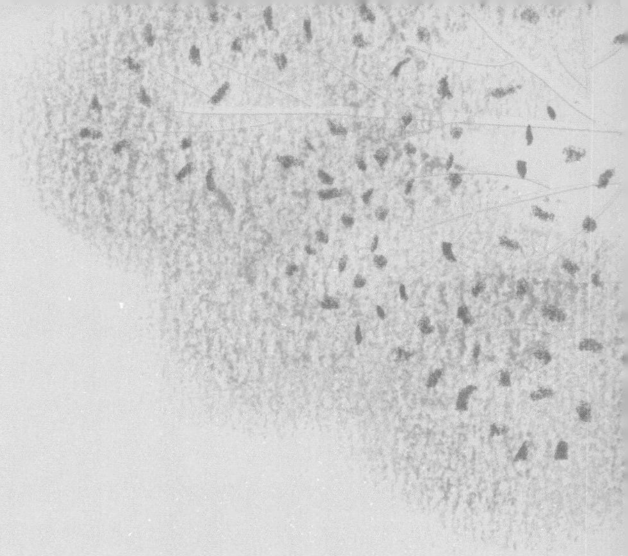
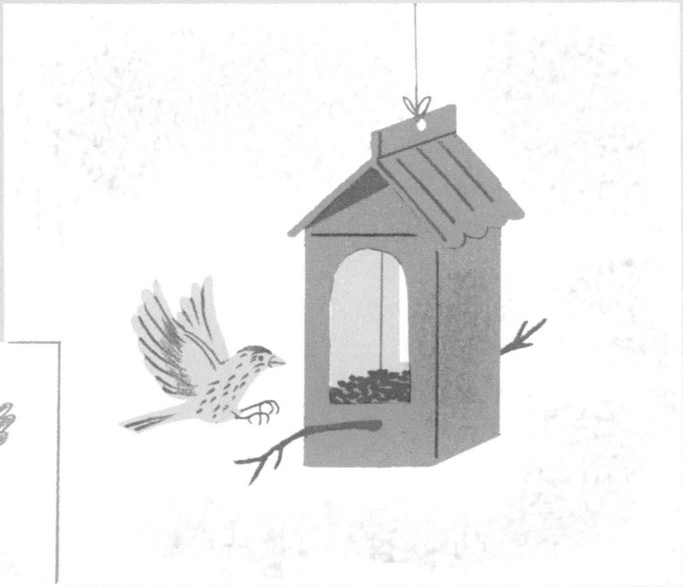
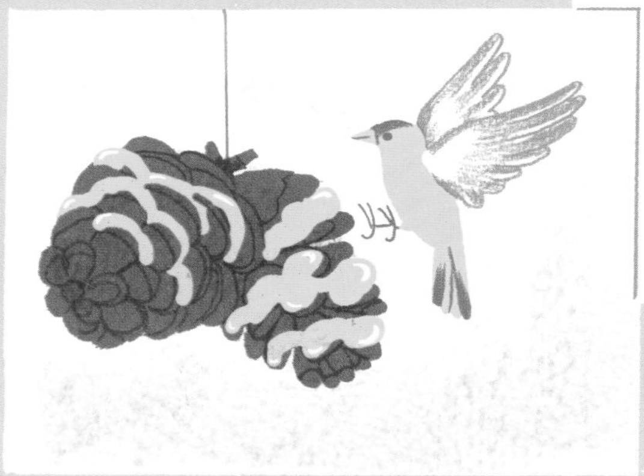

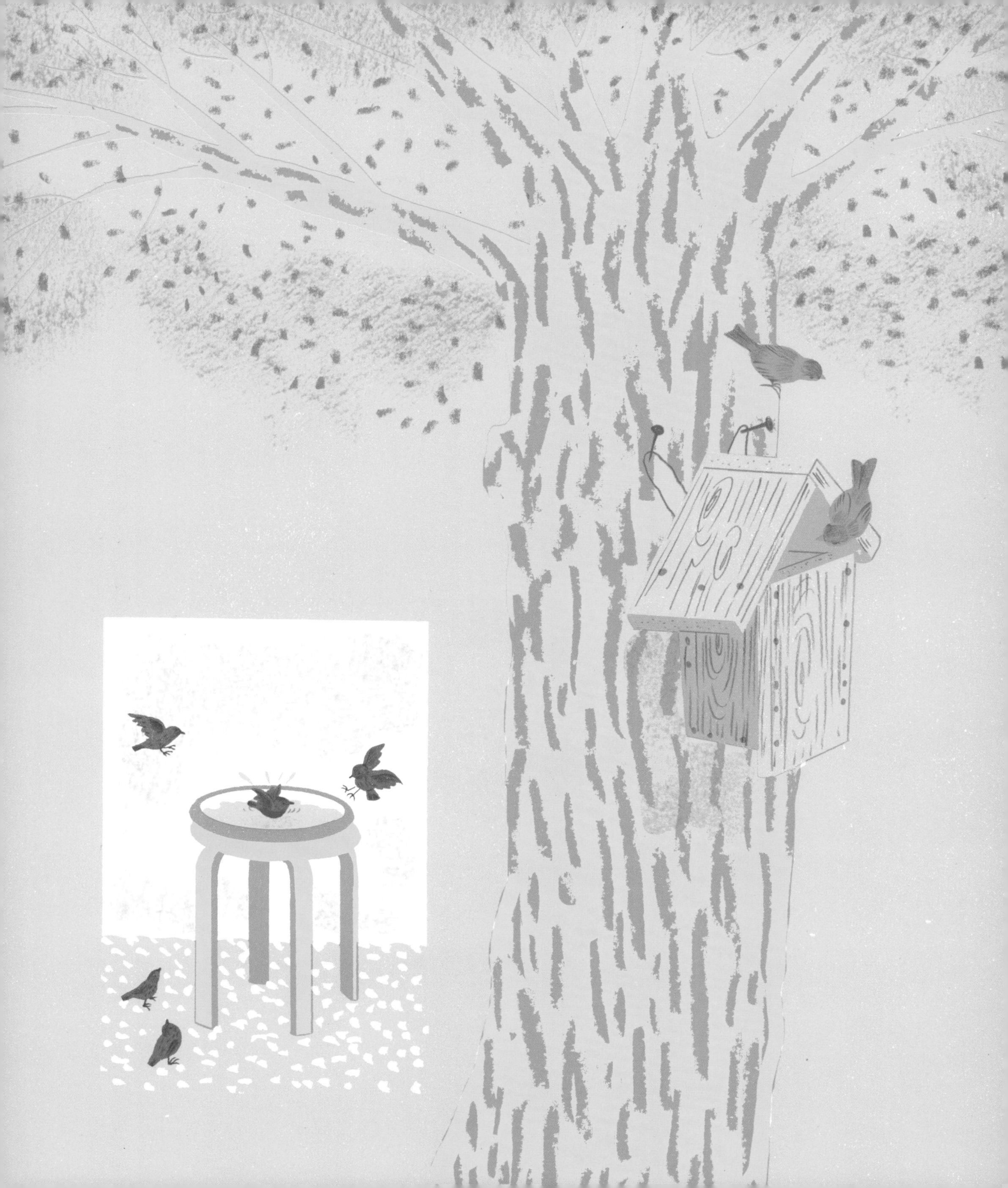

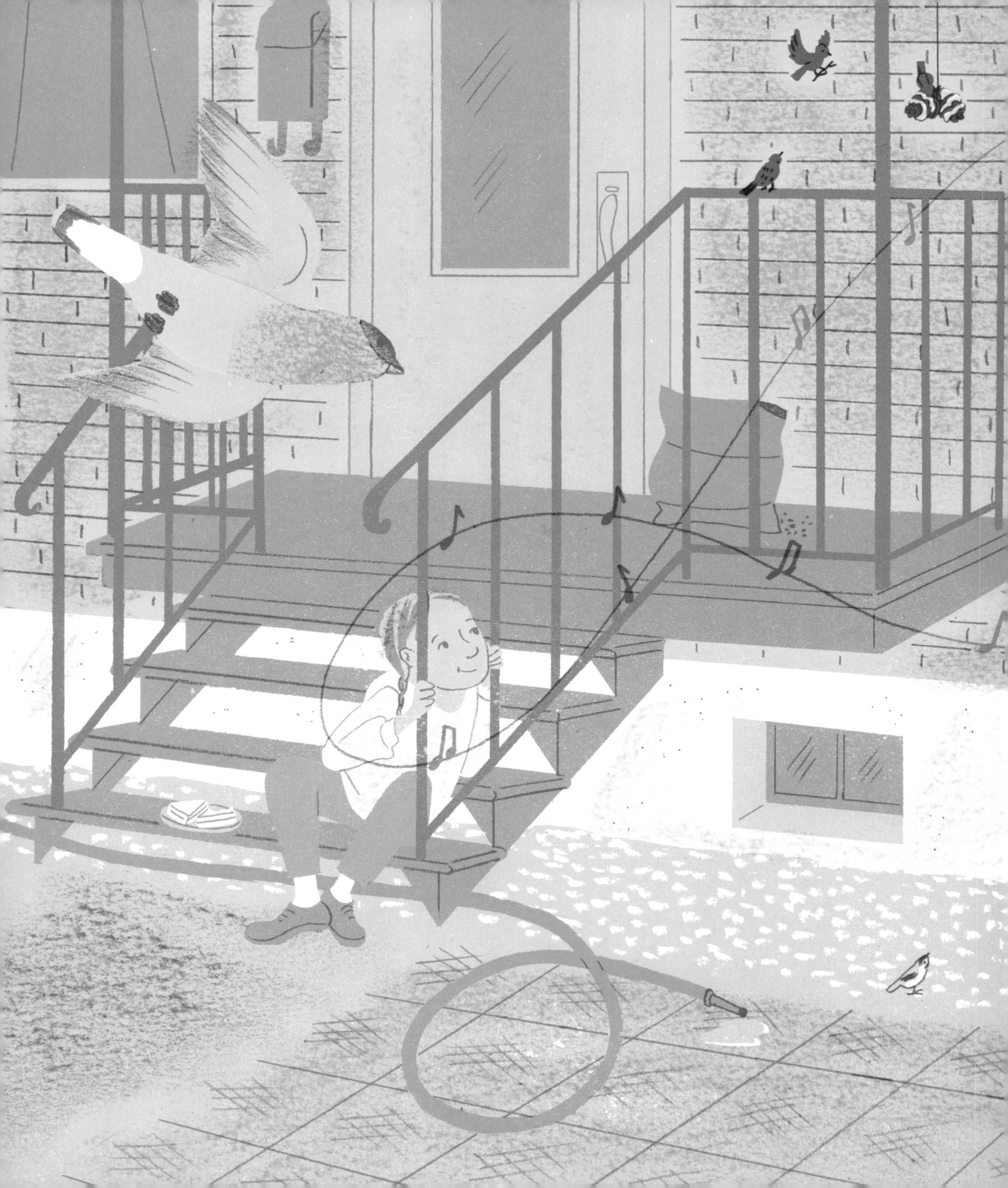

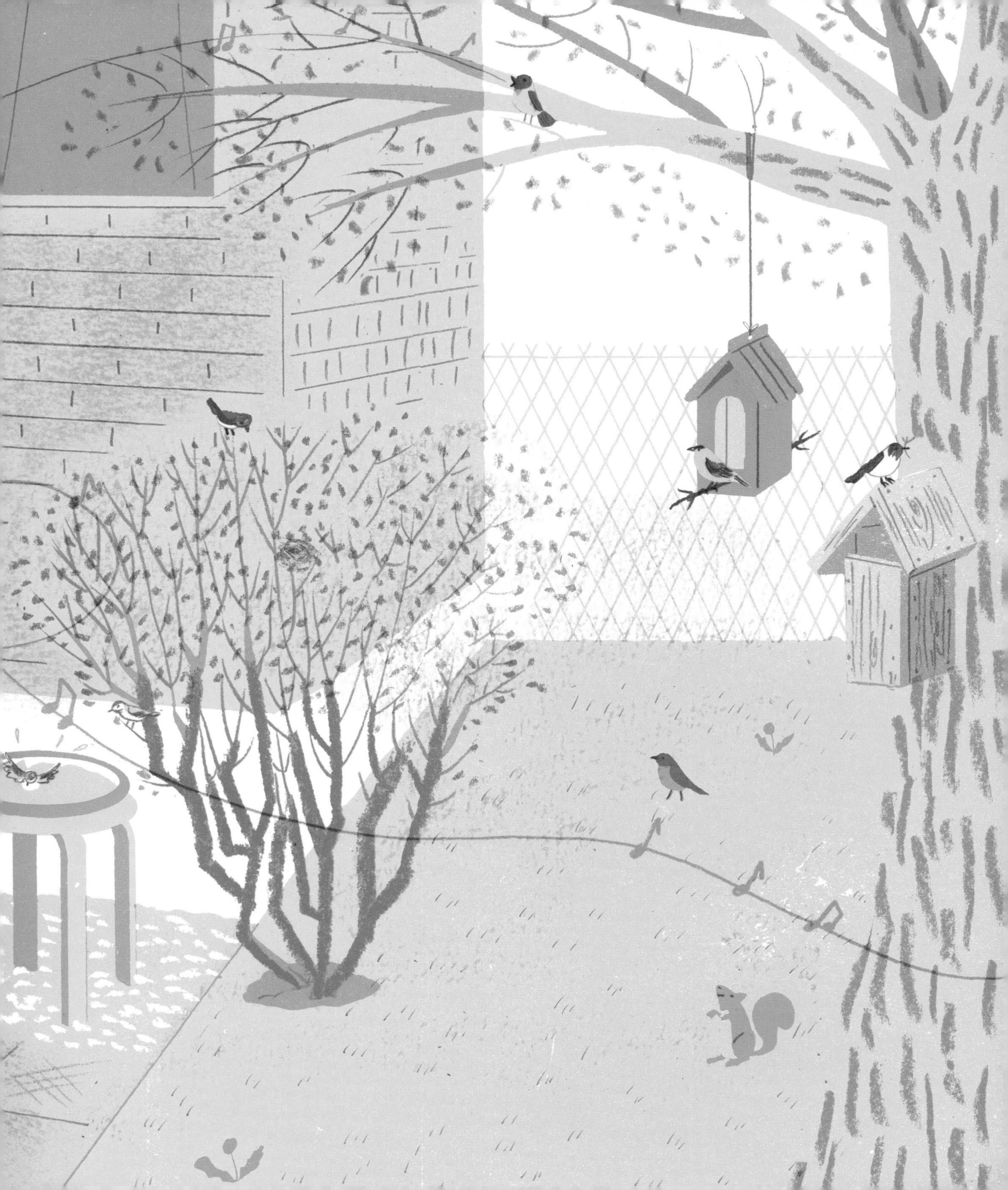

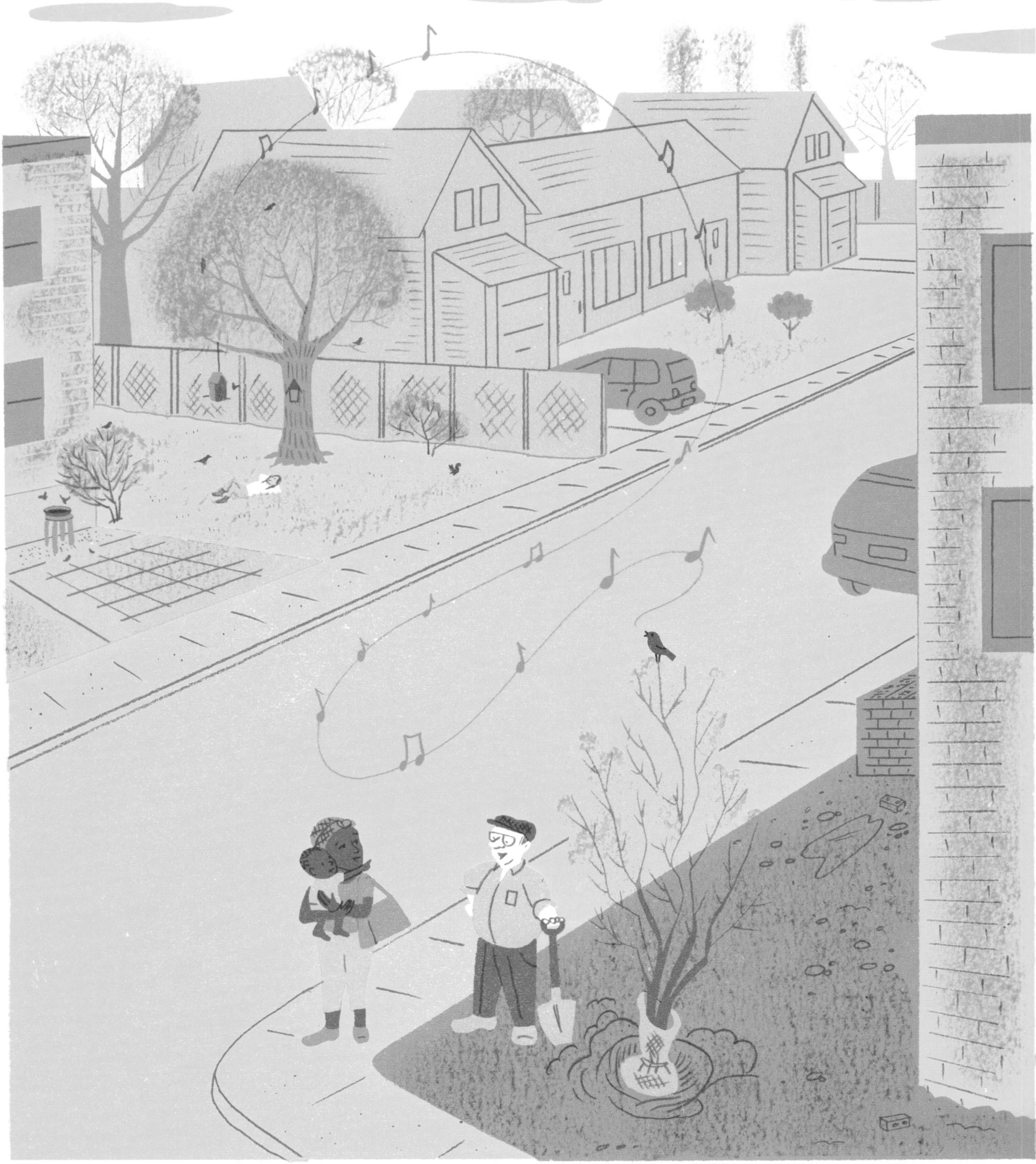